DEVIL'S GRAZE

DEVIL'S GRAZE

WESTERN STORIES

FRANK BONHAM
EDITED BY BILL PRONZINI

FIVE STAR

A part of Gale, Cengage Learning

GALE
CENGAGE Learning

Detroit • New York • San Francisco • New Haven, Conn • Waterville, Maine • London

LIBRARY OF CONGRESS CATALOGING-IN-PUBLICATION DATA

Bonham, Frank.
  Devil's graze : western stories / by Frank Bonham ; edited by Bill Pronzini. — 1st ed.
    p. cm.
  ISBN-13: 978-1-59414-620-6 (alk. paper)
  ISBN-10: 1-59414-620-9 (alk. paper)
  I. Pronzini, Bill. II. Title.
PS3503.O4315A6 2008
813'.54—dc22
                                                    2007038737

First Edition. First Printing: March 2008.
Published in 2008 in conjunction with Golden West Literary Agency.

Printed in the United States of America
1 2 3 4 5 6 7 12 11 10 09 08

TABLE OF CONTENTS

FOREWORD

Before he began producing such acclaimed Western novels as *Snaketrack* (1952), *Hardrock* (1959), *Cast a Long Shadow* (1964), and the posthumously published The Eye of the Hunter (1989), Frank Bonham was a prolific contributor of short stories and novelettes to the Western, adventure, and "slick" magazines of the 1940s and early 1950s. *Devil's Graze* is the eighth collection of his short fiction to be published by Five Star Westerns for the enjoyment of modern readers.

The hallmarks of Bonham's work—a diversity of themes, settings, and time frames, meticulously researched period detail, well-developed characters both male and female, and vividly described action sequences—are amply showcased in the seven stories collected here. "Brides for Oregon" concerns the adventures and hardships encountered by mustanger Hugh Lamerick when he undertakes the dual tasks of driving a herd of horses and leading a wagon train of "strong, courageous young women willing to have a go at settling the West" from Fort Laramie, Wyoming to Portland, Oregon. Dramatic clashes between individuals and armies during the bloody struggle between Mexico and the States for possession of Texas is the strong stuff of "Captain Satan." Vigorous and sharply different, "Devil's Graze" and "Longhorns Are Tough" display Bonham's sure hand with the rangeland yarn. "Hop Yard Widow" is distinguished for its highly unusual background of Oregon's hop fields and for its equally unusual love triangle. The pitfalls of modern-day logging in the rugged Sierra Nevada of northern California form the basis for "The Long Fall." Hero of several stories first published in *Star Western*, Marshal Gus Hobbes, "the most notorious hangman in New Mexico Territory" who will hang anyone for a fee except an innocent man, is at his relentless best in "Hangin' Hobbs's Hemp Stampede," a rousing tale of gold, greed, and gunsmoke.

Readers of Bonham's novels and his previous Five Star collections, as well as those who have yet to experience his exemplary brand of Western fiction, will find much to admire in these stories. For Frank Bonham, like such of his contemporaries as Jack Schaefer, Luke Short, Peter Dawson, and Steve Frazee, was a storyteller of the first rank.

Bill Pronzini
Petaluma, California

★ ★ ★ ★ ★

BRIDES FOR OREGON

★ ★ ★ ★ ★

I

Lamerick took the pipe out of his teeth and said to Sam Tooey: "Got any more of that junk?" Tooey dug in the pocket of his fringed leather coat. He found a necklace of green glass beads as big as penny jawbreakers. Lamerick took it, but did not move yet. He kept watching the Irish girl at the trading post gate.

The girl pointed to the high, white moccasins an Ogallala squaw wanted to sell and said: "Three dollars is too much. Will you take a dollar?"

Lamerick walked to the gate, a big young fellow in a red flannel shirt, knitted silk suspenders, and leather pants. The haft of a knife rose from his right boot and there was a Dragoon pistol at his hip.

The girl started as he looped the beads about her neck. "What are you doing?"

He considered the necklace. "That green glass looks like the devil with your eyes, but it will buy you the moccasins."

"Why, thank you," she said, puzzled.

She turned back, tapped the beads, and pointed to the moccasins again. The squaw passed the moccasins through the gate and the girl thrust the beads at the squaw.

The girl tried to force $1 on Lamerick. He took her arm to guide her onto the parade ground. He hadn't talked to an honest-to-god white woman in six months. He had spent six months buying horses to drive to Oregon, and he had been another six weeks driving them from the Missouri to Fort

11

Laramie, the jumping-off place.

He watched the small, pointed toes of her boots appear and disappear from behind the curtain of gown and petticoats.

"The name," he said, "is Hugh Lamerick. Yours would be O'Hara, or Murphy, something like that."

"Oliver. Irish on my mother's side. Shawn Oliver."

"Wherever your home is," he remarked, "you're a long way from it. New York?"

"Boston."

"Are you for California or Oregon?"

"Oregon."

"Homesteading?"

"We're not sure. Where are you going?"

"Oregon. I own those horses you saw down on the river." Then he recognized the big, harried-looking man she had ridden into the fort with an hour ago walking toward them. "Your husband?" he asked.

"He's Owl Robinson, the boss of our wagon train. Some of our 'whackers deserted and we had to drive back here to find more men."

Lamerick winced. "Lady, there isn't a man in Fort Laramie without plans. Robinson is apt to have to ride all the way back to Nebraska City for hands."

Her eyes came up to his in alarm, but then the wagon master was stopping with a gathered brow and set mouth to stare at them. He was a large man with a brown spade beard and a face grooved with worries. He wore a brown canvas duster over his frock coat and black trousers, and a high-crowned derby sat four-square on his head. His puckered gray eyes exhausted their interest in Lamerick quickly and he stared at Shawn Oliver, storming without raising his voice.

"Not a man to be had! Not one lousy bullwhacker in the post!"

"Why, that can't be!" Shawn exclaimed.

"I talked to the commandant, the sutler, and every man who looked as though he'd be able to rock an ox."

"Then what are we going to do?" the girl demanded quietly, but in a way that put it up to him.

Robinson's eyes traveled about the big, noisy fort. Army wagons rambled through the streets and horses stood at the hitch racks in the astringent sun of late spring. There were the smells of buffalo hides and pine smoke. "Maybe you'd like to suggest something, ma'am."

Shawn said tightly: "We paid you to take us to Oregon. How you get us there is your concern."

Robinson briefly shut his eyes, as a man will on a story heard too many times. He opened them as Hugh Lamerick asked: "Why did the men quit?"

"Because they were trash! Because I was green and took men who merely wanted to get to Wyoming, and were willing to be paid to ride with us." Then his eyes pinched in quick interest. After a moment's sharp regard he put out his hand. "Might I ask your name?"

"Lamerick. I own those horses down at the river."

Robinson's mouth formed into a smile. "You're going to Oregon?"

Hugh read him as plain as a book. Hugh was twenty-four, with a taste for excitement. He had not yet developed a need for responsibility. There was enough grief in driving a herd of horses without throwing in with a badly organized train of emigrants.

"We're for Portland," he told Robinson. "Why?"

"Because," Robinson said, "it appears to me we're in a position to do each other a favor. I need three 'whackers. You may need more protection from the Indians than those horses are going to give you."

Lamerick shrugged. "Big risk, big profit."

"But why take a risk you don't need to? Those twenty wagons of ours make a mighty tight corral at night."

"So do our rifles."

"But can your rifles make biscuits like Shawn here? When it rains, can you sleep under them as you would a wagon? Why, you might say the Lord threw us together to ease our mutual miseries."

Shawn's face had brightened. "It does seem that way, doesn't it?"

Lamerick pulled a red-bowled Indian pipe from his pocket, and slowly shook his head. "The sign's not right. I'm sorry. But I'll keep an eye out for any stray 'whackers. Hope you like the moccasins, miss. Glad to meet you, Robinson."

He was sitting with Sam Tooey and the others when the pair left the fort a few minutes later. They were on the seat of an outrageously impractical vehicle for this country: a topless buggy with an umbrella for shade. The girl sat straight on the seat, but she was dabbing at her nose with a handkerchief.

At 2:00 p.m. a wood-cutting detail rattled in with half-empty wagons. They carried cut wood in two of them and a scalped hunter in a third. Apprehension thudded in Lamerick's head like an Indian drum. He was at the commandant's office when the story came out.

An Ogallala tribe was responsible. There would be a punitive patrol, and after that God himself couldn't take a herd of horses through South Pass safely!

Lamerick gathered his men, fifteen riders from the breaks of East Texas and Missouri. He bulled them out of the post and down to the camp. They had only hit Fort Laramie the day before, and there were many dusty miles behind them. Sam Tooey, a former blacksmith, slung ill naturedly out of the saddle.

"I could be hammering horseshoes at Buff'lo B'ou for more than this outfit pays, and sleep indoors o' nights."

As he outlined his plan to join the Oregon train, Hugh saw the men's interest begin to stretch itself like a wakening cougar. There was hot blood in the crew, and he wasn't sure he liked the risk of worsening matters by exposing the men to a wagon train's half dozen unattached females. Yet he knew now it would be suicidal to go on with no more hope of shelter in an Indian attack than the bodies of his slaughtered horses.

They struck camp next morning. The dirty gray tents collapsed, the fires were scattered, the two wagons were loaded. Lamerick cinched his sack and balanced it on his shoulder.

He gave the men a brusque warning. "I can tell there's going to be a sight of night herding in this outfit. Steal a kiss or two if you feel like it, but let me hear a man sigh and I'll keep him a mile from anything that don't have whiskers. Maybe we won't hang with this outfit long. If we don't, I won't take any of their single females along and I don't want to lose any of you to Robinson."

II

Owl Robinson's train was drawn up in a square of taut gray wagon sheets in the lee of a crust of rocks and brush. The oxen were pastured on a spring branch to the south.

They sat their horses while Owl Robinson, a second man, and Shawn Oliver came from one of the wagons. It was impossible not to notice the prevalence of young women. Yet there couldn't have been better than twenty men here in camp and with the oxen.

Robinson had trimmed his beard and brushed his high flat-topped derby. In the canvas duster and well-rubbed boots he was a commanding figure. He reached up to shake Hugh's hand and introduced him to the other man.

"Gideon Souvran, my assistant wagon master."

Souvran was a lanky, tall man in fringed buckskins, a taffy-colored beard framing his face. His hair was longer than it needed to be, and there was a pampered look about his eyes, and Hugh did not care for him. But he shook Souvran's hand and made up his mind to tell him some things about maintaining a wagon train later on.

Robinson's eagerness surfaced. He gestured at the horse herd on the slope above the camp. "Is this merely a visit or will you join the train?"

"We thought we'd have a try at going double harness with you."

Souvran grinned. "It wouldn't have nothing to do with that skinned hunter they brought in? We seen him on the road."

Robinson's mouth hardened. He disciplined Souvran with a stare. "We aren't concerned with motives," he snapped. "Shawn, wasn't there some of that buffalo hump stew left at our mess? I daresay these gentlemen are hungry."

Young women were drifting near to stare at the mustangers.

Shawn exclaimed: "All they can eat!" Her eyes warmed on Lamerick's stubborn face.

"Where are the men?" Hugh asked.

"Men?" Robinson repeated.

"The husbands. If there's a man for every second woman I see, you've got all the crew you're entitled to. If there aren't fifty women inside this corral . . ."

"Eighty," Shawn said. "You haven't any objection to women, have you, Mister Lamerick?"

Lamerick was staggered. "Eighty! I've seen a lot of wagon trains, miss, but I'll be gol-horned if I ever saw one like this!"

Robinson smiled. "These young ladies are from the East. I'm escorting them to Oregon. If you've ever been to the Coast, you'll know there are ten men for every woman there. Wives are in such demand that . . . well, you can't build a new civilization out of men alone. Now and then an agent is dispatched to the East to find strong, courageous young women willing to have a go at settling in the West. I happen to be one of those agents. Miss Oliver and the other ladies, except for a half dozen or so, are . . . brides for Oregon."

Hugh's knees prodded his pony. He turned the horse and jerked his head at Sam Tooey and the others. Shawn stepped around to grasp his horse's cheek strap. She stood there with one small fist on her hip and her head tilted back. The sharp-edged shadows of the noon sun emphasized the thinness of her features.

"You object to being a party to matrimony on a large scale, Mister Lamerick?"

"Or a small one," Hugh returned. "My business is running horses, not brides. If a man hasn't the get-up to get his own bride, he can't need one very badly."

"Farmers, for instance? They can leave the planting of their crops for a year while they go East and marry the first woman they run into?"

"Well, they'd have a trip out of it, and at least they'd be responsible for their own pick."

"As it happens," Shawn told him, "I did the picking of the ladies for Mister Robinson. Most of them were servants or bond girls, or simply decent young women tired of stitching millinery."

A number of the brides had gathered to stare at the mustangers. Mungo Maroni, the scout, was already in a winking bout with a plump little blonde woman.

Hugh began to smile, appreciating the humor of it. "What happens in Portland? A sack race, with the winner to have first choice?"

Owl Robinson buffed the top of his derby with his sleeve.

"First come, first served," he said.

Lamerick, considering somberly, began to shake his head. "No go," he said. "I'm for getting to Oregon before snow flies."

For an instant, Robinson's puckered black eyes speculated. "I'd like a word with you in private, Lamerick."

Hugh dismounted and followed Robinson toward the center of the corral.

There was no wheedling in Robinson's face. He said shortly: "I don't like to haggle, though it appears you do. If you're holding out for a percentage, I'll dicker with you. I'm to collect two hundred dollars per lady. That would be sixteen hundred dollars. I'll pay you ten percent of the gross for your services. Sixteen hundred dollars for eating riz bread and homemade pickles and sleeping out of the rain. For coming through with your scalp attached."

Hugh scratched his neck. Sixteen hundred dollars would underwrite half his wage bill. He thought of the bag of gold some horse trader would put in his hands for the herd, and most of it clear.

Down in the square of wagons he discerned the light-limbed form of Shawn Oliver carrying firewood to a wagon. She was a provocation to him. She had the temperament of a teamster but the delicacy of a mockingbird.

In the end he said, not fully understanding his own motives: "The sixteen hundred does it, Robinson. We're your men."

The primary thing to be understood about Owl Robinson, Lamerick came to decide, was that his great wagon of ambition was hitched to a sore-footed nag of poor planning. This whole scheme of his was boldly original in conception, but in execution impractical as a left-handed scythe. He had started with too many oxen and too little food. So as the food was used up, he began to slaughter oxen, and, as the badly shod oxen gave out, he made the shattering discovery that he had not an extra draft animal in the outfit.

He had twenty wagons, so he had hired twenty men, plus Souvran, the assistant wagon master who doubled as hunter. Among them there was not a smith, a veterinarian, or a scout. Three men deserted; that had left him with the choice of abandoning three wagons and their twelve ladies, or of finding new bullwhackers. That was the situation when Hugh joined him.

Robinson's manner toward the women was courtly, but faintly contemptuous. He had his mind focused far above them on the sacred mountain called wealth. He was a man of magnificent extravagances, but of scrounging meanness.

On the high sage flats the grass was meager. There was no timber in sight. The country sloughed off in easy rolls, breaking toward the Little Rock, three days' travel ahead. Suddenly they heard the soft pelting of hoofs and a herd of buffalo ambled across a rise directly ahead of them. Gid Souvran's thumb sawed back the hammer of his rifle.

"Luck, by heaven! We ain't two mile from the train!"

The herd came down the break of the ridge, moving with an awkward lunging gait, not running, yet not stopping to crop the tough graze. They were heading for water; the Sweetwater was only a few miles behind. Souvran sat there, contemplating the herd as he might have regarded a quarter of beef in a butcher shop, selecting his cut.

Hugh kneed his pony quickly out of the path of the buffalo. "Ever shot buffalo before?" he demanded.

The wagon boss' stare was quick and ill natured. "Since I was ten."

"Then you ought to know better than to set your horse in their path when the sun's in their eyes. They can't see fifty feet."

Souvran moved aside. The herd was a sluggish flow of thick

19

brown bodies. There were some new calves in the pack, a promise of good eating. Souvran suddenly threw a Rebel yell, put a ball into one of the calves, and spurred up to the fringe of the herd. Hugh swore and bawled a warning at him. What Souvran was doing was all in good buffalo-hunting tradition—starting them on a pelting run to crowd the fattest to the rear and pick them off. But Souvran was forgetting that it was easier to stop the march of a glacier than to turn a herd of buffalo blinded by the sun.

The animals had broken into full run.

Hugh spurred alongside Souvran. "If you want to wreck the train, you can do it easier with a torch! Now, we've got to turn them!"

Souvran knew he had blundered, but there was a stubborn ledge of pride in him that would not acknowledge a fault. He spurred his horse against Hugh's, crowding it away. Above the tawny beard his eyes were pale and hot. "You handle your crow baits and I'll handle the huntin'! If you can shoot that thing you're carrying, stick with me and I'll show you which to kill."

"I'll show you right now! The leaders, and hope the herd turns."

He cut at the head of Souvran's pony with the end of his reins and swerved ahead. He heard the hunter swear, and then there was a brief whistling sound and pain exploded inside his head.

III

He must have fallen heavily, for his whole body ached. He lay there in the short grass with his horse cropping a few rods east. Awareness caught at him and he sat up. His hand found the long welt on his head where Souvran had struck him, probably with a rifle barrel. Then the soft trampling of hoofs came to him again and he rose dizzily to his knees. Distantly he saw them, lunging, dirty-brown, moving across a hill. They were a half mile a way, and the wagon train could not be over a mile. He could not see Gid Souvran; he assumed he had gone forward to try to turn the herd.

Hugh started after his horse, fighting off the desire to shamble drunkenly with his head in his hands. A dull hammer at the back of his head was driving a blunt wedge. He caught the reins of the horse and pulled himself into the saddle.

It was too late. He knew that already. If it were going to happen, it would happen. He hoped Tooey would have time to get the horses out of the path; he hoped the wagon train was headed up. The brutes would overturn and destroy everything in camp if it were still squared. He thought of Shawn, and that was when he sank the spurs in the horse's flank and grabbed the horn to steady himself in the saddle.

A rise swelled under him and the horse came across a ridge, and ahead and below was the blueprint of what was to happen. The buffalo, Souvran racing along before them flapping his hat in their faces, rushed along in a sort of blunted pear shape at the half-formed wagon train. Back on the slope Tooey was flogging the herd to safety. Owl Robinson was leaping from the lead wagon, clutching a long rifle and banging his hat on with a flat smack of his palm. He ran back to crawl under a wagon. The women were out of sight, but Hugh could hear them screaming.

Souvran gave it up. He turned his pony and rode for the slope where the horses were moving up. A moment later the buffalo hit the first yoke of oxen.

It was a quick and brutal thing. The oxen were upended and disemboweled by the short, curved horns of the buffalo. The wagon was hauled half about and overturned. The water barrel split and staves flew like chips. The herd kept on, ripping the sheets off a couple of wagons, knocking off water barrels as they went down the line, and finally straggling off across the hill where the horses had been pastured.

Owl Robinson came from beneath the wagon and looked up the line. Then he turned and stared behind. Finally he began to swear. In the heavy quiet, Hugh Lamerick could hear Shawn Oliver's voice from somewhere, shrill and impatient.

"Mister Robinson! We can do without that sort of language!"

They corralled up where they had spent the last night. In Hugh's herd there were a dozen good draft animals. He cut four of them out and set to work breaking them to replace Robinson's yoke of oxen. Robinson fussed about, mourning over his bad luck. "Blind buffalo! If there's such a thing as flying squirrels on this desert, Lamerick, we'll have a plague of them before we're through. What are those horses going to cost me?" he asked.

"Two hundred apiece. Payable when we get there." Hugh's anger was a tight-mouthed rebellion that was building like a head of steam. Chained to a damned herd of human mares driven by the stupidest men who ever chewed a straw! They'd drag along for a week fighting those green horses, stopping every second day to splint up a crippled wagon. Half the water barrels had been trimmed off their projecting shelves aside the wagons. They could count on some dry camps after they left South Pass.

Souvran found things to do outside camp, skinning out buffalo, stripping jerky. By the time he got in range, Hugh's sense of logic had taken hold. Feuds could be fatal to a train on the long crossing; he could wait for his settlement and let Gid Souvran sweat.

Shawn extended herself to set out a top-notch meal that night, with camp bread baked in Dutch ovens, tender filets of buffalo, and a salad of deer-tongue lettuce she had gathered at the last creek crossing. Robinson finished early and went off to pore over his maps and papers in his wagon. Souvran hung around the back of Shawn's wagon, where she came and went at the sheet-iron stove.

Hugh heard Tooey sigh. With some of his woman fever slaked, the blacksmith began to glimpse what Hugh had been trying to hammer home before. Delays . . . responsibilities . . . aggravations. "Mebbeso," he said, "tomorrow would be a good time to give the hosses a run."

"It's too late for that. We're two weeks out of Laramie now. Until we strike the Coast, the devil holds our mortgage. We can't leave the women to Robinson's blundering."

Mungo Maroni's dark, uncivilized features held the sharp glow of the campfire. He said: "I don't like to think what this windjammer of a wagon boss would do if the women began to hold him back with the weather closing in. He'd junk them and take off in that everlastin' buggy of his for the nearest fort. The hell with the women. He'd look out for Owl Robinson."

Hugh stopped at the back of Shawn's wagon while she was washing the dishes. She had put up her hair in papers and wrapped a cloth about it, Creole-fashion. Her sleeves were rolled to the elbows.

"I'm sorry you had to lend us your horses. But what would we have done without you?" she said.

"What I can't understand is how you got this far without me."

"It begins to surprise me, too." She poured boiling water over the pans and cutlery she had washed. "There's a dish towel there, unless you'd rather watch me work."

Hugh distastefully picked up the towel and began to wipe a tin plate. He wasn't much for scullery work. He tossed it in a box. "There's going to be a lot of disappointed wife-hunters in Oregon," he stated. "There aren't many hired men in that country. Nor bakeries, nor candle makers, nor dressmakers. If a man wants a new saddle or pair of boots, he sets down and hacks it out the best he can. If a woman wants some soap, she makes it herself. How many of these boughten brides of Robinson's would be willing to plow a field if their men got stove up breaking a horse?"

Shawn's gray eyes inspected him critically. "You seem to be a good judge of horses, Mister Lamerick, but a mighty poor judge of women. We have our eyes open. What I want is a house where I'm needed. My own house. I want a house where the kitchen isn't just a crane over a fire. I want a four-poster bed with a goose-feather mattress, and I'm willing to pluck the geese myself. I want a mountain at the back of the pasture and a river at the front. Not a workhouse at the back and a graveyard at the front. You think you're having fun gypsying around, don't you?"

"It beats town life."

"But you don't have to live in a town. Someday you'll be like those old men we saw at Fort Laramie, toothless and penniless, no trade, nothing but guiding they could do, and too old for that. Isn't there any place you ever wanted to stay?"

She had a deep perception, Hugh thought; seeing those old trading post bums always disturbed him a bit. But there was one place he had marked down to come back to someday.

"There's a spot called the Grande Ronde Valley, in eastern Oregon," he mused. "I almost stayed there once. It's farming and cattle and sheep country, however your taste runs. Someday I may go back to stay, when I can't fork a bronc' any more."

He could see that she regarded excessive travel as a sort of sin. "Thank you for the help," she said. "I think we're through now."

About the square of wagons, lamps burned softly against the arched tilts. The mustangers had trailed off to their blankets. Robinson's men were bedding down around the ebbing fires. The air held the pungent fumes of buffalo-chip fires. Shawn had covered the utensil box and walked to the front of the wagon. She raised her skirt a few inches and put her foot on the wagon tongue, glancing at Hugh. "Help me up?"

Hugh took her elbow for a boost. For all her willfulness, she was as dainty as a cliff rose, graceful and feminine. A perverse reaction took place in him. He wanted to let her know she was getting away with it only because of his tolerance. He was still the head of this outfit, even though he had let himself be dragooned into meat getting, selling his horses, and dish drying. That was the pattern his logic took, but inwardly he knew that what he was going to do was only another evidence of her strength and his weakness.

Shawn did not resist him. He brought her down off the wagon in a bear hug. He kissed her mouth. His hand went up into her hair and held her face roughly against his. He might have expected her reaction to be like this. No struggle, no response. Her way of letting him know that he was physically stronger than she, but incredibly weaker morally. He set her back from him. "Payment received," he said.

Shawn's face still held an arch coolness, but there was a hint of humor in her mouth. "What did you expect? If you go out for payment, payment is all you're apt to get. Not thanks."

"I don't want thanks," Hugh returned. "I got myself into this rannikaboo with my eyes open."

She put her hands up on his shoulders again, her hands exerting just a hint of pressure against the hard corners of them. "And that's why I'm really grateful, Hugh. Because you came in with us when you didn't stand to get anything back but the thanks of a wagonload of scared women."

There was that ten percent, which she apparently didn't know about. Hugh did not tell her. She kissed him, slowly and expertly. You never knew about women. They could stand before the whole company looking cool and passionless as a wax bouquet under a glass bell. But the minute you got them alone, the stopper was out; they were impetuous as warm champagne, all pliancy and desire. They were impudent lips and soft arms about your neck. But about that time, if they were clever, they were out of your arms and tossing you a whisper to catch like a rose.

"Good night, Hugh." She mounted to the seat of the wagon, this time without help, and swerved through the canvas cover. He saw her face for a moment, impishly smiling, and then she was gone and a moment later a lamp glowed.

For a second Hugh stood silently. Then he kicked at a scuff of earth, blew out his cheeks, and stepped past the wagon into the darkness. Someone rose from the ground, quiet as an Indian. A man grunted and his fist slanted at Lamerick's face. It hit him on the cheekbone and he went back, caught his spur in the grass, and fell.

Hugh pushed himself up onto his elbows. Gid Souvran stood there. He could see his long face in the gloom, warped with wrath. Souvran's buckskin body was a gray shadow against a black sky.

"Can you read a brand, Lamerick?"

Hugh said—"I can blot one, too"—and lunged up and crowded the hunter back with a swing at his head. Souvran parried it and stabbed at Hugh's jaw. Hugh had his hands locked behind Souvran's neck and brought him forward and down with a swift haul. Souvran caught him about the waist and they fell together.

Hugh lurched up and caught his wrist. On their knees, they swayed against each other. Souvran was a man for choking; his long thumb pressed against Lamerick's windpipe. Hugh began to bend him over backward. He saw his advantage. He jammed his hand into Souvran's face and forced him back on his heels. Souvran tried to twist away. Hugh pinned him flat with a hand on his brisket. He drove to the hunter's jaw and saw his features distort. He battered it with unpitying fury until Gideon Souvran moaned and lay soddenly beneath him.

He got up, feeling the bone ridge above his eye. He glanced about the camp, and then walked on up the hill.

Surfeit of emotion brought its penalty, as did a surfeit of wine. You had to learn to assimilate it. A surly mood was on Hugh at breakfast. He felt like a greenhorn who had been tolled into swilling more liquor than he could hold, for the amusement of his seducers. Shawn's eyes warmed when they touched him; he would not respond. She had enticed him from the status of a teetotaler to that of a drunkard at one bout.

It had been a pleasant sort of drunkenness, but any appetite like that fastened a leg iron on you. It had got him dreaming of the Grande Ronde Valley again. Of a log house and pole corrals, a kitchen garden and thousands of acres of bunchgrass to fatten cattle on. Woman stuff. He curbed himself sharply.

IV

He held this dark-browed mood for two weeks, while the train rambled, with frequent exasperations, toward South Pass. Once they had to improvise a forge and shrink loose tires. They were on higher country, swelling gradually toward a broad fault between the Sweetwater and Rattlesnake Mountains. Snow frosted the ragged crests of the mountain ranges, but below snow line the mountains were blue with timber and the valley was gentle with grass.

No one worked more industriously than Shawn Oliver. She saw to it that the women did not use heat, cold, or discomfort as an excuse for not keeping themselves in trim. One night Hugh heard her holding a beauty rally at her wagon. She talked low, but she talked sternly.

"Ladies, I think we're getting just a bit careless about the curling irons and bleaching towels. We're all getting brown as Bannock squaws. We've got the bleaching towels along for a purpose. Hair can't hang down like horsehair and win a man. It would be a shame to reach Oregon and find we'd lost our attractiveness along the trail."

In a week's time, even Hugh could see the difference. If anything, it made his position more difficult. A troubling intimacy grew between his men and Owl Robinson's girls. There was a little New York girl named Nora Prospect who occupied most of Sam Tooey's time. She was just the girl for Tooey, a meaty little miss with stout arms, shiny brown eyes, glistening hair, and plump hips. She was loud and good-natured, and she was the one who inaugurated the nightly dancing bees. Robinson rode herd on his men sternly, but could not keep them out of it. Hugh did not waste time trying to keep his mustangers away. There was a fight between Mungo Maroni and one of the wagoners over another girl by the name of Sarah Carlin.

On the third morning Robinson wheeled his buggy across the trail that was a half mile wide to where Hugh rode flank on the horse herd, traveling slowly under chain hobbles. Above the spade beard, Robinson's face was flushed. The gray eyes in their pinches of moist flesh were wide and anxious.

"Did you see those smokes in the pass ahead of us?"

"Saw them yesterday."

Robinson fumbled. "We . . . we're going through anyway?"

"Those aren't Indians. That's South Pass City, just a four-bit mining camp. They've been chipping a little gold out of the rocks there for ten years, but they haven't got enough savvy to quit."

It set Robinson back against the padded horsehair seat of the buggy. "A town?"

"You could call it that. Tents, a couple of log cabins, some dugouts. Maybe you'd like to stop and pan a couple of nuggets?"

Robinson tooled the buggy along beside him for a while. "I was thinking . . . I'm short on some things, long on others. Somebody told me to take enough linchpins, and I brought three crates of them. And we've got two crates of clevises and God knows how many pounds of saleratus." He ground on. "I'm going up there. I may be able to trade for some of the things we need."

Hugh watched him seat his hat with a smack of his palm and turn the buggy. "I wouldn't mention the women, if I were you. Not if you want to reach Oregon with them."

Robinson's rutted countenance received it blankly. "No," he said. "No, of course not."

He and Souvran ramped away in the buggy a few minutes later, striking for the cut-off to South Pass City. It was about 8:00 a.m. The train stopped at midday, ten miles from the summit of the pass, and that afternoon threw off by a little mound of rocks that indicated the summit. The valley was so wide and gentle that a traveler seldom knew until he dropped down to Soda Springs that he had crossed the summit of the Rockies. Up here the wind was fresh and strong, whetted on the sharp teeth of the range. Robinson and Souvran whirled in an hour before sundown. Stock was tended, the oxen neck-yoked together for the night, the horses picketed. Supper fires burned ruddily on the grass.

Robinson assembled his crew of eighteen men after supper. He stood on the tongue of his big blue Schuttler wagon with a canvas sack in one hand. He was a bull-throated orator, a crowd catcher, and he was in good spirits.

"Men, we've had it tough up to this point. I allow there may be worse ahead. But you've stuck with me. The dross was burned out at Laramie. The gold remains. Gid and I scouted

South Pass City today. It's a dandy little layout for a man to lose the kinks in. The arrangement," he said sententiously, "was that you were to receive wages in Portland. However, I thought you might like twenty dollars apiece here. There's a canvas outfit called the Bucket of Blood up there. It's not much for looks, but I've drunk worse whiskey in Saint Joe. You can walk it in an hour and a half. Take your money and shake a leg!"

Hugh watched him fling the gold pieces with cautious abandon. It was out of character, like a preacher telling a salacious story. Souvran stood with him, subaltern beside his general. He had drawn into himself since his fight with Lamerick. He seemed to realize the next move was up to him, but it was a big one and he was not ready to make it. The bullwhackers, coats thrown over their shoulders in anticipation of the sharp night chill, deserted camp. Owl Robinson, coat tails flipped back, hands in trouser pockets, watched them go, smiling. Finally he walked over to Hugh. He struck his palms together and rubbed them briskly. "Lamerick," he said, "we're in luck. This is trail's end!"

Hugh squinted at him, and said: "It used to end at Portland."

"For you," Robinson said, "it still does. For me . . . man, when those miners heard we had single women with us . . ."

"I thought you were going to keep quiet about that," Hugh snapped.

Robinson tossed a big, broad palm. "Nobody could have kept the secret. That camp needs women. The meals they eat a starving hound wouldn't touch. The place is filthy. All they've got is gold. Oh, it's no bonanza. But they've been in there, some of them, for three years, and nothing to spend the money on except when they dodge over to Fort Hall once in a while."

"You'd sell the girls into a place like that?"

Robinson bunched his brows. "The point is . . . it won't be like that long . . . not after the ladies take over. They'll pay me more money than I could realize in Oregon. Not only that, but they want to buy every scrap of food and equipment in the wagons. Even some of the wagons themselves."

He gave Hugh a chance to speak, but Hugh looked at him pensively and contained his thoughts. The other rocked back on his heels and stared up the darkening slope toward the mountains.

"It seems fair that you should have five percent for your help. Ten would be steep. Gid and I will slope on over to California with a few wagons. You and your men will be free to go on without us to weigh you down." His eyes came fully, with grave good will, upon Hugh, and he put out his hand. "I want to say, Lamerick, that I appreciate the help you've given me."

Hugh reached up and took the soft knot of his stock in his hand. He twisted it until the collar bit into Robinson's thick neck. "Compared to you," he said, "the Sioux are milk-fed missionaries. You know damned well what would happen to these women up there. They'd get scurvy and lice and freeze for lack of clothes. They came out here to find homes!"

Robinson breathed deeply. He struck off Hugh's hand. "When I want horses," he said, "I go to a horse trader. When I want advice, I go to myself. If I need your advice, Lamerick, I won't hesitate to ask, but it will be about horses. You can cry over it all you want, but the deal is made. The men are coming down tonight to claim their brides."

Hugh's mouth dried. "How many of them?"

"About fifty. The other girls . . . well, there are plenty of lonesome soldiers at Fort Hall."

Hugh was shocked and frightened. Not about Robinson, but about fifty men he had never seen, fifty miners coming to claim the brides they had put out gold for. Or had they? There was a difference in the way a man fought for something he owned and something he aimed to dicker for. He angled into it carefully, trying to keep a step ahead of the promoter.

"It's to be cash on the barrel head?"

"To both of us."

"The same price on all of them?"

"One price. Two-fifty."

"Then they haven't put up their money yet?"

Robinson saw his blunder. "It's as good as if they had."

"The hell with that." Hugh snorted. He turned and called: "Shawn!"

She came from her wagon after a moment. Nora Prospect and Sam Tooey were with her, and Tooey had his arm about Nora's waist. Shawn had her own reserve up since Hugh had failed to follow up his advantage the other night. "What is it?" she asked.

"Robinson thought you might like to marry into South Pass City, instead of Oregon. There are about half enough miners to go around, but not a decent house in the camp. No rugs, no store, but probably plenty of whiskey and lice. Do you want to take a vote among the ladies?"

Shawn turned to Owl Robinson. "You aren't serious?"

Robinson hung onto the soiled lapels of his frock coat. "I wouldn't put it quite the way Lamerick has. It's your opportunity to miss a lot of grief on the trail. There are all the incentives to building a home here that there are on the Willamette."

Shawn's palm found his face with a nonresonant *smack*. "Mister Robinson," she said, "I've thought all along you were operating this enterprise like a carnival promoter with a cage full of freaks. I'm sure of it now. You can ride back up there and tell your miners you've changed your mind."

Robinson clung doggedly to his one advantage. "They're on the way! I can't stop them now. And, besides, it may be that after you meet the gentlemen you'll feel different."

Shawn said: "I saw to it before we left that every lady brought a firearm of some sort. If those miners come into the wagons tonight, I don't think there will be many who carry off a bride."

Hugh watched Robinson join Gid Souvran and saw both men climb into the blue wagon and a lamp come on. Hugh rounded up his own men. Three were riding herd, and that left fourteen for the job ahead. Tooey had his own idea about how to handle the crisis.

"We used a trick in the Mexican War to shake a spy loose of his tongue. Lash a man to a wagon wheel and let 'er roll. A mile, the saying went, would wring a secret service roster out of a general. Robinson ain't a bad 'un, just foolish. He'd be a lot less foolish when we cut him down. So would Souvran."

"That don't help the women much, does it?"

Maroni's dark fox-face narrowed. "Fifty miners . . . I can handle six. How about the rest of you?"

It began to appear, then, that there would be not enough miners to go around. Hugh sat on them, when they began rubbing the handles of their Colts. "Most of you," he pointed out, "would be in this crowd coming down the trail, if you'd been up there panning mud for two or three years. Well, lay it on the line for them before we cut loose. Tell them it's off and send them back. If they don't go, there're enough bullwhips in camp to take off a yard of hide per man. Get your whips, boys. We're going up to meet them."

The trail was a faint trace through rocks and brush. Night was not far off as they slung toward South Pass City on their horses. They stopped in about half an hour and built a fire of dead sage in the middle of the trail. They were warming themselves when the tramp of boots and a ring of voices came to them. They faded back from the fire and stood scattered in the clumps of brush, all but Hugh, who remained there with his bullwhip coiled over his shoulder. The miners came out of the

gloom, a ragged, excited platoon of men tossing jokes and frag-
ments of songs. A big red-shirted man with pants too short and
sideburns too long was in the lead.

He dragged to a halt, staring at the figure beside the fire.
Hugh's rifle was under his arm; the stock of the whip dangled
by his hand. He regarded the troupe in frowning silence. The
other miners fell silent as they saw him. Finally the man in the
lead moved up, his countenance cautious.

"Lookin' for the Robinson train," he said.

"It's gone on," Hugh said.

A frown caught the man's brows. "Divvil, you say! We was to
meet Owl at the camp tonight. We just passed his men."

"He played you for suckers," Hugh said. "He had no right
agreeing to sell the women to you. He didn't mention he had a
pardner, did he?"

The red-shirted one said: "That's you, eh? Well, your quarrel's with him." He started forward. Hugh let the whip fall from
his shoulder in a heavy black coil, supple as a rattlesnake.

"I can't sell the ladies down the river just because you're
lonesome. If you want wives, send your own agent for them.
There's no way out of this for you but to go back. We can't even
sell supplies to you, because ours have to last as far as the
Coast."

All the men were armed. A few carried rifles or carbines, but
most wore revolvers. The man with the sideburns suddenly
stepped back, his hand dropping to his gun. Hugh's arm rolled;
the whip picked itself up off the ground with a hiss. He hurled
the thick lash at the man. It wrapped about him with live
resiliency. He hauled back on the blacksnake. The man's sleeve
ripped and blood spurted from his arm. He groaned and
clapped a hand to his torn forearm.

Sam Tooey walked in from the right and laid it on another
miner who began to show interest in his gun. Maroni brought a

half dozen mustangers from the left and they hacked at the thick mass of men with whips that *whistled* and *popped*. Hugh dropped his whip and raised his rifle as a promise to other men who might go for their guns. The crowd of miners numbered closer to sixty. They fell back, grubbing for rocks to throw, breaking from the ranks and lunging at individual mustangers. They had heard about bullwhips, but they didn't know they could be handled as artistically as a gun, and as painfully. The rawhide poppers tore out clumps of beard and hair, cut white skin under thick shirts with the tearing force of dull knives.

The red-shirted man had his fill. He pushed both arms in front of him and staggered back. "Keep the damn' wenches!" he yelled.

The population of South Pass City went back to their empty town and niggardly sluice boxes.

V

Owl Robinson's train wound down from the pass onto the sagebrush flats. Distance obscured the Tetons. They camped one noon on the bank of the Little Sandy, filled all water barrels, watered the livestock, and through the night crossed the desert between Little Sandy Creek and Green River. It was a desolate and waterless desert where even the sagebrush barely survived, the kind of plain that bent a man's thinking to spots like the Grande Ronde. Hugh's mind fondled that great green bowl fenced in by high mountains. Snows seldom reached it, and in winter the elk came down in herds to graze. The camas flowers glowed pale blue on the ground and the roots of them made the best-eating sweet potato this side of the Mississippi.

A defensive reaction set up in his head. He began to fasten disadvantages onto the valley. Indians were thick. The valley was too far from anywhere. He began to have a mild contempt for the place his thoughts were always pulled back to.

Souvran continued to avail himself of Shawn Oliver's good will. One night Hugh was passing the girl's wagon when he came upon them in the shadows outside the square. Shawn's back was against the wagon and the hunter's hands encircled her slim waist. The ground was soft and absorbed the grind of Hugh's heels. He stopped, and saw Shawn thrust at Souvran and turn her face away.

Her voice was half laughing and breathless when she said: "Gid! I declare you're the most impatient man who ever lived."

Souvran's tongue was thick with emotion. "Anybody'd be impatient, Shawn."

"But this isn't even Idaho yet. I said when we got to Oregon I'd think about getting married. . . ."

Then she saw Hugh and her gasp turned Souvran to face him. Hugh walked on.

He told himself she was of no importance to him, and yet he felt the sickness of jealousy in his heart. Through that night he considered taking his horses and pulling out. But from here the trail was devious. There was the crossing of the Snake, simple if you hit it right, tragic if you missed. And there was the Modoc trouble that had been going on in eastern Oregon.

He came into camp early the next morning, planning to take a chunk of camp bread and jerky and eat in the saddle. As he was grubbing in the food box, Shawn appeared with a scarf over her head. He started past her, but she caught his arm. "Hugh!"

He faced her with hard, unshaven features. She was turned toward him. "I know what you thought last night. Hugh, you're wrong,"

"I was wrong," Hugh said, "about the kind of train this is. You didn't have to go to Oregon to make friends like Souvran."

The camp was still quiet. She looked at him with slow hurt in her face. "You can't quite see our position, can you? No man could. I thought we had a friend at first, even though you were so contemptuous of anything a woman could offer in the way of real help. At South Pass I was sure of it. Sometimes I still am. But you've done everything you can to make us realize you may ride out and leave us any time you decide you've had enough. And if that happens, we know how long Robinson would stay with us. He's got a heart like an accountant's head. He knows how much it costs per day to feed us, and he's going to have to replenish nearly everything at Fort Hall. He knows that by the time he reaches Portland with us, he'll do well to break even. Hugh," she pleaded, "the only reason he doesn't abandon us, or dump us in some hole like South Pass City, is because of you."

"Isn't that good enough for you?" Hugh asked.

"It is while it lasts. But Sam Tooey told Nora he thought you were about fed up. That you might pull out with the horse herd any day."

"Maybe he's right."

He was merely extracting revenge for the night before. But the color came angrily into her cheeks and her lips firmed. "That's exactly why I've encouraged Gid. If I could split him and Robinson and keep Gid on our side until we reached Oregon, he'd make Robinson stay with us if you didn't."

Hugh laughed. "It explains how I came by that kiss so easy."

He strode off through the wagons. A sense of shame robbed him of any triumph.

The trail to Oregon was comprised of hardships and monotony. Three islands—harbors of safety, supplies, and gossip—rose out of this vast sea at almost equal distances: Fort Laramie, Fort Hall, and Fort Walla Walla. Laramie was behind. Fort Hall, the big Hudson Bay Company trading post in the Snake River Valley, was coming up out of the distant haze. The bullwhackers all spoke of it, the mustangers had their mouths set for whiskey, their fists set for scraps with the fur trappers coming down to rendezvous.

Robinson absorbed all this talk. It was his first time over the trail, as it was for most of them. For him, Hugh knew, it was a dismal as well as a pleasing prospect. He had supplies to put in for at the fort, smithing to be done, animals to be shod, wages to be doled out to his bullwhackers. He must outfit here for the long swing across the Snake and around the Blue Mountains to Fort Walla Walla. Here or at Fort Boise, farther down the Snake, where supplies came even higher.

He was ready with a new suggestion one night. "Miss Oliver," he said, "according to my map we should be at Fort Hall in three days."

"That's right," Shawn said.

"They're beginning to farm near the fort, I have heard," Robinson said. "They say there's a fortune in raising truck to sell to the fort. It occurred to me. . . ."

Shawn said sharply: "You contracted to set us down in Portland. You will not get rid of us one mile this side of it."

Robinson said: "I've seen short-sightedness before, but never in such quantities."

In the morning, Hugh noticed that Souvran was gone. They had plenty of fresh meat and jerky and it was obvious he would not be hunting. There was somewhere else he could be, and that was on the trail to Fort Hall, to make arrangements such as they had made at South Pass City, but taking greater precautions this time.

About noon they struck a small side trail. Hugh said to Robinson: "You can cut out a couple of river crossings this way. Better graze, too."

Robinson decided to try the short cut. They were on it four days. Finally he came to Hugh in frowning impatience. "I thought you called this a short cut."

"It is a short cut. To Fort Boise. We'll be there in another twelve days."

Anger suddenly tightening his face, Robinson produced a double-barreled Derringer. They were alone at the front of the train, where Hugh was mending a piece of harness during the noon halt. It was all as Robinson might have prayed for. There was no one within fifty feet, no one watching, no one to deny his story that he had caught Hugh poking in his wagon and had been forced to throw down on him. Then the gun slipped away and Robinson dropped it back into a big square pocket of his coat.

"This is a business with me," he said. "You've tampered with it twice now, and for the last time. The next time it will be as though I caught you in my strongbox. How I manage my train will be no concern of yours after today. You can travel with us or not. You can pull your men off the wagons, if you like. The women can double up with the others."

It was a waiting game. Souvran caught up with the train at Fort Boise with a lame excuse about having tracked a herd of antelope until he got lost. Robinson bought supplies scantily, despite Shawn's protests. "We'll re-outfit at one of the Oregon forts," he told her.

Hugh said: "The Oregon forts are Army forts. They don't sell supplies."

Robinson and Souvran collected every item of information about the trail ahead from the trappers at the fort. Hugh stuck close. They learned that the Oregon volunteers had cleaned up the Modocs and were waiting for their discharges. The trail to the California mining camps took off just beyond Fort Cayuse and was in good condition. Robinson's eyes sharpened. It came to Hugh that Robinson had torn his gaze from Oregon, that he had damned the whole territory as a jinx and thrown the weight of his promotional scheming in the direction of the gold camps.

They wound northwest from the Snake through the Wallowas. Hugh watched the landmarks pass with greater interest. One day they would come down through a pass, suddenly, and see the Grande Ronde below them, whispering with summer grasses, populated by a few settlers, a couple of forts, and great herds of elk. He clung to his device of contempt for its softness, like a woman's lap, fit to dandle a kid in but not fit for a man.

Very suddenly he was robbed of that self-imposed lie.

They came through a pass one afternoon and saw the valley below them to the north, filled with a purple haze and backed by the Blues. Snow marbled the peaks, drenched with the sunset. Far north of them a blur of smoke lay on the valley floor. Robinson hunched forward on the seat of his buggy. Souvran drove Shawn's wagon, and they all watched Hugh study it. Hugh turned his horse and rode back; the horse herd had gone on down to the campsite on Currant Creek.

Robinson asked quickly: "Grande Ronde Valley?"

Hugh nodded. It was pure foolishness; the mere sight of the place set his heart to pounding. It bred in him a feeling he had never known—the sensation of homecoming.

"Fort Cayuse is at the head of it," he said. "You can probably buy some supplies there. We'll throw off tonight on Currant Creek. It's a full day to the fort."

He rode on back. The pink opalescent light of the sunset was on Shawn's face. Her bonnet hung down her back by the strings and both her hands lay limply on the seat, as if the sight of that glorious valley were something magical. It made Hugh turn to look at it again. He heard her say: "It's the Grande Ronde, Hugh. I know it is!"

Hugh said roughly: "And all cluttered up with settlers since I was here last. I can see three cabins from here."

He rode on down to the horse herd, in the lower foothills. The wagons came in at dark. There was the bustle of watering stock, neck-yoking them for the night, cutting wood and build-

40

ing fires, minor repairs to wired-up contraptions of wagons. But Hugh sensed that Owl Robinson and Gideon Souvran were not taking part in it. They stood off at the fringe of the activity, and the talk between them was heated. He had a swift recollection of Shawn's declaration of strategy: to split them up and have at least that protection. Then they broke off and Souvran went to rig up the sheet-iron stove for the girl, while Robinson stood with his hands in his pockets trying to pierce the darkness.

They were in Oregon at last, but they were still two months from Portland. Two months that would rob any profit he made from the expedition. The California trail cut due west from Fort Cayuse. Hugh thought: *If I know him at all, it will happen there.* He would not lug those eternal females another mile. He would dump them at Cayuse for whatever salvage value they might have with the Oregon volunteers, and leave them stranded.

But Hugh told himself it was no business of his. They could worry it out.

Then he looked about camp and saw them at their work, industrious as ants, and he had a sharp pang in his heart. They had been through a lot, and they had taken it well. They didn't cry over the dry scrapes or complain about weevilly flour. Shawn did all that for them, but even her fretting was a sort of business gesture. All of Robinson's complaining was based on the fact that they could not harness a team and they were costing him money to feed.

The responsibility of them sat on Hugh's back like a bale of furs. It crushed out his delight in entering the Grande Ronde. It suffocated his dream of trail's end at the Willamette. He walked down to look at the horses. The young night was warm, full of the odors of camas and sticky laurel, tender with bunchgrass under foot that cured like domestic hay. It was the best feed in the world for livestock.

He stood there and tried to project himself across the Blues, the Wallowas, the Cascades, down into the gentle valley of the Willamette, where Oregon City and Portland waited to ease the travel kinks out of a man. He found it impossible.

Then he knew what had happened.

Shawn had pushed him unwillingly into the room called maturity. He'd found some responsibility, and he could never lose it again. A youth could do selfish, harebrained things and be smiled at. A man, doing the same things, earned the contempt of other men.

Dimly he was aware of a kinship between himself and Owl Robinson. Robinson was still riding the rainbow roughshod, panicky when he thought he was going to be dragooned into something he did not want to do. Hugh had turned over and over in his mind, like a coin, the thought of what must be done when the climax came. Tonight was the climax. Tomorrow night, at the fort, might be too late. He knew what had to be done, and he was ready to do it.

Dinner was ready at his mess. Robinson and Souvran had eaten hastily and disappeared. He ate, and hoped no one saw him stuff three extra pieces of corn dodger and a handful of jerky into his pocket. A man could work up an appetite on a thirty-mile ride. He rose lazily to his feet and sauntered across the square. He heard someone following and glanced back. Shawn, her face taut with alarm, walked beside him for a moment.

She said: "Hugh, I'm not asking for help. But be on your guard. Souvran demanded an answer tonight. Would I marry him, or wouldn't I? I told him I wouldn't. I don't know what they're planning, but if he was ever in my camp, he's back in Robinson's now."

Hugh reached for her arm as she turned, but she eluded him and ran lightly to the wagon and busied herself at the stove. He was ashamed of his whole relationship with her. She had been acting like a woman; he had been acting like a beardless Don Juan, finding his satisfaction in hurting her.

Unhurriedly he reached the corral line of parked wagons and stepped across a tongue in the darkness. He found Mungo Maroni with the saddle horses, going over his pony with a dandy brush before turning it into the remuda. He tugged at the latigo of his own horse and spoke quietly to the mustanger.

"I'm going up to the fort tonight. This time we're going to steal the march on them."

Maroni's fox-like face studied him. "What's the game, Hugh? You're going to sell them out before he can?"

Hugh bridled, but after a moment turned back to the horse, knowing he had let himself in for it. "No. There's a lot of lonesome farmers and cowmen and God knows what at that post, volunteers that never wanted to fight anyway. I'll bet most of them would pay five hundred dollars for a wife to take back with them, if they had it. What'll they do when I tell them the girls are willing to be courted at Owl Robinson's camp, and it won't cost them a dime, if they can talk the girl into it?"

Maroni's arm dangled laxly with the brush. "Now, how do you think you're going to sell Robinson on that?"

"I've sold myself on it. He had his money for transporting the women, and I don't figure he's entitled to anything for bringing them through. I'm riding up to invite the men to meet us halfway."

He reined the bay into the darkness.

He had gone about a quarter of a mile when he heard hoof beats. He stopped and listened. Elk. He could hear them *clattering* through a stream. Filled with confidence, he rode with no particular caution, so that when riders came at him, two from each side of the trail, it was a thing as astounding as sun at midnight. A rider's arm rose and something hacked at his head. There was a brilliant explosion of fire behind his eyeballs, and then the night flowed into his brain.

VI

When he struggled to consciousness on the cold beach of misery, there was only one man with him: Owl Robinson. Robinson sat there in his high politician's derby and canvas duster, regarding him curiously. There was something sad in Robinson's expression. Hugh tried to sit up and found his wrists and ankles lashed together behind his back.

"I'm afraid you'll have to stay that way," Robinson said.

"I expect so," Hugh said. "So you were on the road, too."

Robinson frowned. "I don't see what you hoped to gain by this."

Pain rose and fell in Hugh's head like tides. When it was high, he was blind with it; when it ebbed, he was aware of nausea. He said nothing, and Robinson sighed.

"It was a sorry day for both of us when we teamed up. At least you got us through the mountains. I'm leaving the ladies here, of course. They'll be in good hands."

"Maybe. That's what I was riding to see about myself."

"You hadn't," Robinson suggested, "any idea about my commission?"

"I had an idea of letting the girls decide that. You've tried to dump them in every human cesspool between here and Laramie. If they wanted any of the volunteers, I wanted them to have fair choice. It's not how much a man would pay for a woman, but how much love the woman had for him."

"Love?" Robinson laughed, a cynical sound in the night. "Is there some chemical that will breed love overnight?"

"No. But there's a chemical, whatever it is, that breeds it in a couple of months, sometimes. My idea is to camp here until the men get their discharges, prospecting around a little, putting in camas roots and elk meat and berries and the like. So if it

44

doesn't take, the ladies can still go on to Portland."

"But whatever their pick, Owl Robinson is out of it, eh?"

Hugh closed his eyes, drowning in a surge of pain. A few minutes later he realized Robinson had moved, that he was on a horse and he was talking. "I'm sorry," he said. "The men wanted to kill you, but . . . well, I've got ethics, though you might not think so. Or say I'm like the king who hadn't the heart to lop off a man's head. So he cut it off an inch at a time. You're far enough off the trail I don't think you need to torture yourself about hope of being found. I expect they think you're at the fort, anyhow. I wouldn't do much shouting. They couldn't hear, but the animals could."

Afterward, it was like a little nightmare his mind had looked at, and lost in a pool of darker dreams.

He tried to fight the thongs, but had no success. Then he decided simply to rest, not allowing himself to think about cougars, and in a short time he was asleep. Dawn was eating at the black horizon when he awoke. He saw the prints of large paws in the earth near him. Bear or cougar. But they were fat on fawns and tender, early-summer things, and hadn't dared to touch the mysterious thing lying in the thicket of serviceberry.

Ants and flies began to worry him. He went into a fit of tugging at the thongs again. Thank God, it didn't feel like rawhide! Rawhide, if it were green, shrank in the sun until it could strangle a man's limb and blacken it with gangrene. The Indians knew all about that. He suspected he was tied with saddle strings. Then after quite a while, with the sun up and birds swimming in the deep blue sea of sky above him, he heard hoofs again. Deer? Elk? Antelope? But they had a hard iron ring, and he rolled over to face the noise and commenced shouting.

It made no difference if it were Robinson. But it might be Sam or Maroni out hunting him. Why? They wouldn't expect him back for hours yet, and no doubt Robinson had carried him up a stream or two to lose tracks before dumping him here. And then, all at once, he was looking up at the ugly little face of Sam Tooey, with its brows like hedges and his mouth wide enough for two men. Tooey smiled wryly.

"Hugh, you damned fool." He swung down.

Someone else pushed a horse through the brush, and there was Shawn, wearing someone's borrowed buckskin breeches and a leather shirt. Her hair had been shaken out of its customary tight knot, and she sat there and her face dissolved into broken lines and she began to cry. Tooey lingered to stare at her, puzzled.

"He's all right, sis. What are you crying about? He ain't dead." He scratched his head.

She held out her arms and the blacksmith helped her down. She was so stiff she had to hobble to Hugh's side, and there she sank down by him and held his face in her hands. She tried to talk, but her voice soared into a choked little wail and she buried her face against his neck as Tooey cut the thongs. Hugh put his arm around her; it felt thick as a log.

After a moment, Sam grunted: "This ain't decent."

"Then don't look." Hugh sat up and held her on his lap, her head against his shoulder, his hand stroking her face. He was corralled. Her brand was burned on him in characters a foot high. But he knew there was no freedom in the world to compare with belonging to someone who needed you. He kissed her, and for a moment, before Tooey spoiled it, it was like the night in camp, that spilled-champagne feeling again. . . .

The mustanger turned his back. "And Owl Robinson riding hell-for-leather with the light cavalry at his back, to steal our women!"

The situation called for prompt action.

Shawn pulled away. She looked at him in a way no woman had looked at him before—possessively, as though she owned him, but was the weaker because of it—and she seemed trying to remind herself that they were still on the crest of a crisis. "That's right, Hugh. His 'whackers all deserted last night. Your horse came in and we knew something had happened."

Tooey grunted. "They were cagey as all hell carrying you up here. Crossed two streams, riding half a mile up each one to shake us. But they packed you across your own horse, and turned him loose, or he got loose. He was back in the herd this morning. He came a little more direct."

Hugh washed in a stream, soaked his head, and had to rest a while. They had brought his pony along, and he mounted after a few minutes. "Now, what about it?" he asked Tooey.

"Well, I figger he isn't going to slip this time. He's taking cash at the post, or dickering for it. And if them Oregon sons-o'-trappers put out money, they're going to demand value received."

"And that isn't the way it was supposed to be at all," Shawn protested. "We were to camp at Portland and everybody would know why we were there. We wanted husbands. But they'd come with flowers in their hands, instead of a receipt. And we'd be the ones to do the choosing."

They broke through the serviceberry thicket onto a deer trail. "And that's how it's going to be," Hugh stated.

"But if they come back with him . . . maybe a hundred of them! And there are only eighteen of you."

"What do you think?" Hugh asked Tooey. The mere act of riding made his head pound, without trying to think.

"You're supposed to be the think department," Tooey retorted.

Hugh did think, and by the time they reached camp, an hour and a half later, he was ready with something.

VII

Camp had been made in the wide cañon of Currant Creek. The walls of it stair-stepped back in ledges of rusty rimrock. Yellow sage and buckthorn grew thickly in the mouth of the cañon where it fanned out into the valley. They could see little of the valley floor, but Mango Maroni, acting as look-out on the point below, was ready to pass the word up. About 3:00 in the afternoon he rose up and shouted.

"My God, boys! A whole damn' troop o' cavalry!"

He came running up the ledge of rock he had laid on. Presently the *thud* of hoofs came to them. Sam Tooey ran into the brush and flopped behind a clump of sage. Hugh stayed back. He saw the horsemen appear in a solid column. Then they broke apart and spread into a skirmish line on order of a big uniformed man with Owl Robinson and Gid Souvran.

He was the only man wearing a uniform in the lot.

Robinson, Souvran, and the troop commander jogged on in. Tooey came to his knees and let himself be seen, and the uniformed man wheeled his horse on its hind legs as if to rejoin his troopers. Robinson thrust an arm at the smith, not seeing Hugh by the blue Schuttler wagon.

"Not a bit of use to it, Tooey! There are seventy-five men with me. We're here to free the women."

Tooey laughed. "So it's freeing them, now! Lieutenant, how much did you pay for the privilege of freeing one?"

"Colonel," the big man snapped. "Colonel Townsend. I . . . why, that's a matter between Mister Robinson and myself. Give up the women, man. Give them up without a struggle, or we'll be forced to put you out of the way."

"They aren't here, Colonel," Tooey said. "We told them you were coming, and they get so fearful of being saved by a troop of Oregon cavalry that they took to the woods! The rest of the boys are with them."

Souvran kneed his horse forward. "If you've hurt the wenches, you'll answer for it!"

"We ain't, and nobody's going to. Ain't that right . . . Hugh?"

Hugh started from the wagon. He saw the impact of his appearance on Robinson even from there. He seemed to set like cement, his big body not stirring in the saddle. Hugh kept walking, weaving through the gray tufts of sagebrush.

"If you've got any money down, Colonel," he said, "you'd better get it back while you can. There's no need of payment. The ladies came to Oregon to marry, despite Robinson's trying to dump them in every mining camp and regular Army fort we passed. They're waiting in the woods for us to thresh this out."

Robinson spoke rapidly and urgently to the colonel and started forward with Derringer held muzzle up. His face was thick with angry color. Hugh kept walking, and he did not stop speaking. Behind the colonel, the volunteers were worming through the brush, dismounted, the horse holders running back with their mounts in case of action.

"The ladies want husbands. They aren't for sale, but they can be courted."

Colonel Townsend drifted forward. "What's that?" The stiffness began to leave him.

"We intend to camp near the fort while the stock rest," Hugh went on. "If you aren't too busy fighting Indians, we've got a fiddler in the crowd, and a concertina. You never know what will get started in a schottische."

The colonel laughed. "No, sir, you never do! Mister Robinson. . . ."

Robinson shot him a whetted stare. "I've told you the straight of it. There's a contract in my wagon to prove it. I'll not be lied out of what's coming to me."

Hugh said: "No, nothing under the sun will save you from what's coming to you." He stopped there and waited for Robinson and Souvran. Souvran had stopped, but Robinson kept jogging forward. He didn't like an action like this, but he knew which doors were locked to him and which one was still open.

Robinson suddenly flung himself off the horse and shouted back at the troopers: "Forward! Take them!"

He threw the gun at Hugh. Back of him, Gideon Souvran was resting the barrel of his carbine on his elbow. Hugh dived. Souvran's gun jerked; the ball troweled along the ground beside Hugh and spat gravel in his face. Tooey fired once and Souvran doubled up in the saddle. He tried to ride it out as his pony began to pitch, but he came loose in a moment and flopped on the ground.

Robinson let his shot go. It was an earnest attempt, but it passed a yard above Hugh. Hugh was not accustomed to missing a target as big as the promoter, and Robinson was half the size of an elk. He put a bullet into the middle of his chest. He cocked and aimed and fired again, and Owl Robinson slipped forward and put his arms about the horse's neck as though to hang on. The horse began to run and Robinson fell, one boot catching in the stirrup. The scared horse went pitching down the bank of the creek with the big sprawled body bounding along beside it.

The colonel stayed out of range. He looked vastly displeased. He pointed at Hugh and shouted: "Drop your gun, sir! I realize you were fired on, but there will have to be an investigation. If what Mister Robinson told me was true, you're in trouble."

Hugh holstered his gun. Maroni and Sam Tooey looked back at him and did the same. The Oregonians closed in. As they drew within fifty feet, Hugh saw that they looked just as he'd hoped they would, like farmers, tradesmen, and artisans. Good husband material. Most of them were young and raw-looking, hard and earnest. He let the colonel take his gun, and he smiled as he did.

"Will you take the word of eighty young females over one burned-out rake like Owl Robinson?"

The officer's hard mouth broke. "I'm afraid I might be inclined to. He took two hundred dollars from me and an I.O.U. for fifty more. I thought that I.O.U. was going too far."

"You could buy a section of good land with two hundred and fifty dollars, Colonel."

"A section! Why, God, man. . . ." He had to stop and shake his head. "Land is cheap as dirt here, and there's more of it than there are people. Settlers . . . that's all we need. We've got the finest farm land in the world on the Willamette, the best cattle in the world on the John Day."

"I know," Hugh said. "Every man's got his favorite spot. Mine's the Grande Ronde. Right under your feet. I'm settling here, with one woman, a hundred and fifty horses, and more hopes than you could shake a Modoc Indian at."

A polite man, the colonel turned to regard the valley. "Yes, it can hardly be beat anywhere. That's for sure. I wish you luck." He began to rub his hands together. "About the ladies, now. . . ."

"Oh, yes," Hugh recalled. "About the ladies. . . ." He turned to get his horse, and they all rode up into the timber, tucking in shirt tails and looking down critically at their shadows as they rode.

★ ★ ★ ★ ★

CAPTAIN SATAN

★ ★ ★ ★ ★

I

Colonel Jabez Stout had been too long a border soldier to possess anything like tact. Moreover, he had had too many years as ranking officer of the Second Texas Dragoons to be greatly concerned about tolerance. But his affability, as he faced Standage in the lamplit office, might have deceived a man who had not been at swords' points with him a dozen times in this same room.

"A pity to disturb you at this unholy hour," he said. "I thought it best, however, that you hear Corporal Reagan's report. Afterward I shall be glad to have your suggestions. Out here, Mister Standage, we blunder along so."

Stout's ram's-horn mustaches and peppery hair were still sleep-rumpled. His dark-blue trousers were, as always, out of press, his black Jefferson boots badly stirrup-marked, and a gray undershirt with elbow-length sleeves was the only covering for his bone-rack chest.

Captain Standage said nothing. He had a close grain that the colonel's finest shafts failed to penetrate. But neither he nor the corporal missed the irony of the situation.

Corporal Reagan paused to eject tobacco juice onto the hearth. He was a crusty regular who had been in Standage's command at San Felipe, a Roman-nosed knout of a man with insolent brown eyes and red sideburns.

"Well, sir," he said, feeling his importance a little, "I cut sign on a parcel of horses and wagons south of Parras. There was no bottom to the mud down there . . . hadn't stopped raining in two weeks . . . and those wagons were traveling heavy. I judged from the number of horses that they were traveling with a big escort. That meant a supply train . . . powder and ball for Cholo's guerrillas along the Bend. The wagons went north as far as Río Amargo. Piedras Ford was also out there, and the river was lapping her banks. There was nothing for them to do but hole up and wait for the water to go down. I found them camped outside Villalobos, twenty miles west. I figure they won't be able to make the crossing for three days yet."

Reagan's slate-blue jacket was unbuttoned and he tucked his hands in the hip pockets of his mud-spattered trousers. He let a pause gather, his eyes finding those of Captain Standage.

"I got close enough to see their guidon," he said. "It was yellow and green, with some kind of red doodad in the middle of it."

"The Maguey!" Colonel Stout remarked. "Hidalgo's Lancers, Mister Standage. Apparently they mean that supply train to get through."

Standage had expected a surprise of some kind—the setting bristled with potential. But at the mention of the name, Hidalgo, his stomach muscles tightened. He stood very still, a lean, dark-blue figure sketched against the whitewashed adobe wall. He had crossed Hidalgo's path before—but that was in 1836, in San Felipe, before the Mexican dubbed himself a general and built an army equal to anything along the border in the bloody struggle between Mexico and the States for possession of Texas.

Reagan was watching him. Reagan had a stiff knee and a lance wound in the shoulder that dated back to San Felipe, and he had a fistful of grievances born in the same hour in the bloody battle.

Standage was conscious of the colonel's gaze. He had his foot on a chair seat, elbow on knee, chin against fist. One eye was closed and the other, squinted, gleamed like polished bluestone. The silence deepened.

It was Stout who said at last: "Well, Mister Standage . . . ?"

"Well, Colonel?" Standage crossed his arms.

"I asked for your suggestions," the colonel said. Rancor was coming out on him like the hackles lifting on the neck of a pit bull.

"I prefer that the colonel plan his own campaign."

Stout straightened, the blood coming into his face. He was finding Standage a poor butt for his joke.

"Very well, Mister Standage. It should be plain even to an infantryman what should be done. We must strike Hidalgo with every man and horse we can spare before he can cross Río Amargo. If he makes rendezvous with Cholo, it means the end of our northern supply line for months. But, unfortunately, you have made such a move impossible."

"I, Colonel?"

Stout was suddenly barking, his temper running free. "With your everlasting drill, and inspections, and patrols! With the hour crying for action, you bring your men in from a four-day reconnaissance patrol, worn to nubbins and unfit for combat!"

Standage said sharply: "My men will be ready to take the field in an hour."

The colonel flung the chair aside. "You are not only a brass-and-fluff parade-ground soldier, but a fool as well! To save your own face you would send those men out to be butchered!" He took a snorting breath through his nose. "You have not changed, I perceive, in ten years. You are still Standage, of San Felipe."

Reagan was watching the infantry officer with the greedy enjoyment of a belated pleasure in his face. But the coldness was gone from Standage's manner, and his words were short.

"I do not see where I am required to save face. I have given the men what they needed . . . hard work to make hard men. I took them over softer than recruits. In two months I have made seasoned soldiers out of every one of them."

"There is a difference between seasoned soldiers and mutinous, exhausted ones." Pride came into Stout's voice. "I have campaigned on the border for ten years, and in that time I have not put my dragoons through an hour's drill. Off-duty, they are scoundrels and hoodlums. They drink and they brawl and they chase the girls. General Taylor called them 'The Magnificent Drunkards.' But we win battles! That is all I ask of any soldier."

He yanked a heavy shirt from a wall peg and commenced shrugging into it. "Since Russell's death . . . God rest his soul! . . . you have turned what was a crack battalion of Foot Rifles into the bedraggled carcass of an outfit. You may call them seasoned troopers, Captain. I call them armed coolies."

"That point can best be settled on the battlefield," the captain said coldly.

Stout ceased buttoning the shirt. "That was my own thought," he said. "You will turn your men out at dawn, Mister Standage. Draw rations for six days and issue full combat equipment. We will see how many of your foot soldiers are on hand to watch the Second Texas flush Hidalgo out of his rat's hole."

Standage would have left then, but the colonel stopped him.

"I noticed a book on your desk while you were on patrol. Something about the logistics of modern warfare. If you can balance that volume on your saddle horn as you lead a charge, Mister Standage, I shall recommend that you be decorated for distinguished juggling while under fire."

The bugler sniggered.

Captain Standage went past the sutler's store and up the wide alley between the low adobe barracks and the shambling buildings of laundry row. The black wing of night was still over the garrison, but dawn was not far off. He could hear the men snoring as he walked, the vigorous snoring of men who have earned their sleep. They would grumble when Corporal Reagan's bugle roused them, but after the kinks were out, they would be ready for a march and a fight.

They had been rotten with liquor and idleness when he had assumed command. Standage had taken their whiskey from them and given them drill. Walking along the alley, close to the wall, he knew they hated him for many things. For forced marches and short rations. For stormy bivouacs and long nights of sentry duty. For making soldiers out of them.

He felt their hatred when he rode at the head of the column down heat-choked arroyos. It was in their faces at retreat, when they stood woodenly at parade rest in the short, dark jackets and sky-blue trousers of the Fourth Foot Rifles, that had not been brushed or washed for months before he arrived.

Martinet . . . ? He wanted his men to fight like devils and behave like gentlemen. Yet he knew he could have bought the respect and friendship of the men under him years ago, had he been willing to trade for these things his own dearly bought convictions. But he had set his star by those beliefs too long, had paid too much in the learning of them.

Once he had overheard Sergeant Major Ramsay telling the story to a gang of recruits.

"I'll tell yez the trouble with Mister Standage, my lads, and it'll be costing the lives of some of us one day . . . he sets more store by a campaign ribbon than he does the lives of his men. Reagan learned that at San Felipe. It was his bugle sounded the charge that threw a platoon of our Foot Rifles against two troops of Mexican lancers. What happened? What could happen! He was trying to save a handful of cannoneers the greasers'd cut off, but he lost most of his own command, instead. Here's a promise, lads . . . you'll travel to hell and back before you find a colder-hearted devil than Standage, of San Felipe."

In the dusty-black dawn, Standage sat his horse beside the colonel's at the main gate, feeling the lift of excitement as the sounds and odors of the combat detail swirled about him. H and J Troops, the colonel's pride, centered by with sabers and carbines *clanking*.

There was little precision to their movement, and the captain had a moment of warmth when his own detail marched by at quick-time, musket barrels canted at the measured angle, boot heels striking the ground in cadence. He felt a rich satisfaction, not that he had bent wills to his, but that he had sweated the indolence out of them and given them a hardness that would serve them in battle.

Stout said—"Take charge of your detail, Mister Standage."— and loped to the head of the column, stretching out down the long, curving road from the hill. As the train of supply wagons jolted through the gate, Standage took his place beside his men. Reagan swung in, whistling under his breath.

Neither B Troop's Lieutenant Pierce nor D Troop's Lieutenant Barney had had much to say when he had announced what the patrol involved. But Mr. Barney, who was young and chunky and who possessed, besides some mulish ideas of his own, a pair of magnificent black sideburns that curved scimitar-like to the corners of his mouth, had remarked: "You think the men are capable of a forced march, sir?"

Standage said dryly: "I think they are soldiers, Lieutenant . . . not school boys."

In the growing light they strung out along a freshet-swollen arroyo that led them southwest, holding this course most of the morning. The sky, which had been cloudy for days, cleared off in the afternoon. Overhead the sun flamed with an ardor that brought the sweat soaking through the men's jackets. Standage had no anxiety for musket-sling sores. His troop of rifles had slogged through hotter days than this, if they had never resented a march more.

He felt the rancor of their glances every time his eye ran down the long column shoving doggedly across the broken wasteland. Yet with a certain smugness he noted that the "Magnificent Drunkards" were reaching for their flat wooden canteens more often than was healthy.

They left the sage land for an arroyo-riven waste that crumpled far ahead into a chaos of flinty mountains. Standage, discerning a piping of green along the foothills, said to Reagan: "Río Amargo, Corporal?"

The bugler nodded. He was riding with a knee kinked about the swell of the saddle, bugle slung under his arm. "Piedras Ford is south of the saddle in the hills yonder. Villalobos is eight hours' ride from the ford. But we'll do well to make camp along the river tonight."

Ahead, the colonel's bay gelding swung from the point of the column. Stout raised his hand, a lanky, high-shouldered figure erect on the saddle. The non-commissioned officers sent the command down the line like a volley of rifle shots: "Detail . . . halt!"

Standage loped ahead. Stout looked ill tempered and hot. He had not ridden combat patrol in many months, and Standage guessed he was finding the saddle less pleasant than a chair on the gallery with a long drink in his hand. Sweat had soaked the stand-up collar of his blue frock coat. Sweat was on his red bony features and in the frayed mustaches.

"Devilish poor progress we're making, Captain," he said shortly.

"The colonel is setting the pace," Standage remarked with a

critical glance for the lathered, blown mounts of the Second Texas.

"Never mind the horses," Stout snapped. "They will not be the ones to break down. What concerns me is that we shall be making camp near the river without having scouted the *bosque* for *ambuscaderos.*"

"Then we should have started an hour earlier," Standage pointed out.

"A little late to think of that," said the colonel acidly. "I propose to take the mounted detail ahead and choose a campsite before sundown. You will continue on to Piedras Ford. Is that clear?"

Standage nodded. "Quite clear." What was not clear was how the horses would hold up at a canter when they were clearly bogging down under a walk.

II

The sun had plunged behind the saw-tooth hills in a rosy spray of cirrus clouds when Standage led his weary troop of Foot Rifles into the humid green bosque of the Río Amargo. The smoke of supper fires was a tang in his nostrils. They passed a sentry leaning against a cottonwood. By the sounds and the flash of the fires through the trees they located the troops in a large clearing, cross-hatched with rows of pup tents. Among the trees the horses, ridden half to death, were being tended.

Standage turned his troop over to Lieutenant Pierce, and, with Mr. Barney, sought the colonel. Stout was in front of his own tent under a tree, drinking noisily from a canteen. Observing the burned-out look of him, the captain knew this day had levied heavy tribute on his strength.

Stout lowered the canteen, mopping his dripping mustaches with his free hand. He saw the infantrymen, and the expression that surged into his face somehow startled the captain. His lips made a smile, but it had cruelty.

"Foul luck, gentlemen," he said. "It appears your march has accomplished nothing more than to wear worn boots thinner. Have you inspected the ford?"

"You mean . . . they have already crossed?" Barney asked, startled.

"That," said the colonel, "is exactly what I do not mean. I am saying that the ford is still flooded. That the wagonloads of supplies you must carry to be of any use to me whatever cannot be forded across for days."

Standage looked at him. Without a word he set off toward the river. Stout and Barney, following, found him standing on the crumbling bank, watching the muddy current carry away, clod by clod, what had been a jetty-like affair of logs and dirt.

Stout studied him but could not read his face, and presently he said: "My dragoons shall do well to cross, let alone infantry and wagons."

"The colonel is right," said Lieutenant Barney bitterly. "This was an undertaking for dragoons or voltigeurs from the start."

Standage spoke sharply. "Never lose faith in your weapons, Lieutenant. When you do that, you cease to be a soldier. We will cross in the morning."

"But, sir . . . !"

"We will lash logs to a dozen wagons and construct a pontoon bridge," Standage said. "As for supplies, we will drop the blanket rolls and take emergency rations and all the powder and ball each man can carry. Combat packs, Mister Barney. Have them made up tonight."

Stout made a choking sound in his throat. "Hell and damnation! You can't fight a battle on the amount of ammunition each man can carry. You'll not have enough for an assault or a siege."

"Then," said the captain, smiling, "we shall have to thin our powder with sweat, shall we not? And if we run out of powder, we will use steel."

Stout's gray head moved from side to side. His voice was angry and yet it held something of awe. "Mister Standage, I should not care to lay my head on your pillow tomorrow night," he said.

"A man lives by his lights, sir," Standage said softly. "If mine fail me, I shall not need a pillow tomorrow night."

The crossing was made in the first golden flush of dawn. Beyond the bosque the freight trail left the lush bottomlands, ascending the mountains through a wilderness of giant and dwarf pine. For five hours the patrol struggled through forbidding mountain passes.

At length the trail brought them to the mouth of a pass overlooking a broad plateau. Here Reagan announced: "If you sniff hard, Captain, you can smell 'em. Villalobos lies just across the plateau."

Standage passed the word to Stout. Beside a great slab-like boulder the officer dismounted and followed the bugler's directing finger.

"With your glasses you can see them camped in the trees at this end of town. Must be twelve hundred of them . . . infantry, artillery, lancers."

It was Mr. Barney who growled: "Correction, bugler. They were camped at this end of town. There's no sign of them now."

Stout snorted. "Then he's gone soft in the head since the border campaigns, for he's left his wagons behind. They're ringed up in the plaza."

Mr. Pierce, sounding relieved, chuckled. "Evidently he has no stomach for a brush with the Second Texas! Strange, though, that he made no effort to evacuate the wagons. . . ."

Standage was frowning through the glasses, analyzing the approaches to the village: a brown-and-green patchwork of farms;

a meandering stream spanned by a stone bridge; a belt of maguey and paloverde that merged gradually into the trees and box-like *jacales* of the town.

"Apparently," he remarked, "he also neglected to evacuate his artillery. You will notice a number of redoubts on the far side of the barranca. . . ."

There was the stiff silence of surprised men taking a second, closer look. "Captain Standage is right," the colonel said. "We shall not be cheated out of our fight. Mister Standage, Mister Culley . . . have the men drop their packs and all excess equipment. We will advance in combat formation."

As he mounted his horse, he gave Standage a cold smile. "You will not need the supplies you left behind, Captain. Tonight your rifles dine in Villalobos . . . as guests of the Second Texas!"

Excitement ended the grumbling of the troops. Bayonets flashed in the sun as they were fixed to the muzzles of the long rifles. Stout led the descent from the pass. At the bottom the dragoons moved out in double file. The sun was at zenith, its rays running like quicksilver down the raised sabers, shining greenly on the cornfields ahead.

As they passed the first scattered huts, movement could be discerned in the trees across the barranca. Stout saw this, and he came up straight with his nostrils distended, like an old war horse scenting a fight.

From one of the redoubts there was a flash and a black roll of smoke. The ball landed in a cornfield, cutting a crazy swath as it came bounding toward them. With the roar of the first shot still on the air, the remainder of the dozen old field pieces opened up.

"As skirmishers!" Standage snapped the command, and Reagan's bugle came smartly to his lips.

Stout was close enough to bring the flat of his hand against the bell of the bugle. "I will give the orders, Mister Standage!"

"Am I to let my men be cut to pieces?" Standage demanded.

Colonel Stout brought his saber from the scabbard with a flourish. His smile had a bristling ferocity.

"Your men will not come within range until those pieces have been silenced. You are about to see a practical demonstration of the superiority of the dragoon over the foot soldier."

He wheeled his horse. Solid and fused shot were raining down, filling the air with shrapnel and dust. "Mister Culley!" Stout called. "Prepare to storm the redoubts left of the bridge. I will take H Troop against those on the right. You, Mister Standage, will hold your command in readiness to charge after we have taken their cannon and engaged the lancers." His voice strengthened, going like a bugle-note through the troops. "Prepare to charge!"

The dragoons went with a drum roll of hoofs and the cheers of the infantry to speed them. But Standage's face, as he rode to the point of the column and directed the formation of his skirmish line, was stony.

Under the belching mouths of the cannon, the dragoons crossed the stone bridge and swarmed through the first line of redoubts. From the trees a volley of musket fire rippled, cutting a dozen men from the saddle. Standage watched the red guidon of the Second Texas sweep on, through smoke and dust. He saw the Texans' sabers flash and heard their cries as they took the rock fortifications.

A moment later the guidon fluttered on a rise beyond the second line of artillery, and he knew the "Magnificent Drunkards" had made good Stout's boast. Luck, the guiding angel of foolhardy soldiers, had taken them farther than Standage had dreamed they could go.

Feeling the savage spirit that surged up in the men, Standage raised his saber high.

Cannon sound, throaty and startling, arrested him. Without understanding, he watched the fluttering guidon go down, saw sections of the line collapse like ninepins on a skittling field. Chaos attacked the dragoons; in confusion they began to mill.

Mr. Barney shouted: "My God, sir! They've another line of cannon in the trees!"

Standage's arm let the saber descend. A treble chorus of musketry mounted over the kettle drumming of the artillery as the enemy infantry came swarming out of the trees. The Americans were suddenly falling back, the officers screaming orders, the men valiantly trying to pull the raveled fabric of their line together.

And now, with the stage set for slaughter, the Mexican lancers swept out, a yelling circus of shining lances and multi-colored haberdashery—red, green, and yellow uniforms pointed up by gleaming brass. At their head rode a huge-bellied man on a white stallion, a brown giant festooned with gold braid.

Upon Standage's senses the scene laid a clammy sense of familiarity: the little coffee-colored horsemen with their lances leveled across the ponies' heads; the screaming rabble of infantry swarming along behind. But the cries he heard were from the lips of men dead ten years, and the panic rising in him had been born on another field than this.

Against the Mexicans' steel-tipped lances, the dragoons' sabers were flimsy toys. Revolvers came out of bearskin holsters and *crackled* briefly, then the moment cried for retreat or massacre. They *clattered* back across the bridge, a ragged ghost of the force that had gone out so gloriously.

They had put a precarious 100 feet between themselves and the Mexicans when they regained their own lines and swept around the flank. Lieutenant Pierce came up, white to the lobes of his ears.

"Sir! Are we going to let them be slaughtered? A charge,

perhaps . . . ?"

"A heroic thought, Lieutenant," said Standage, "but not tactically sound. Corporal Reagan will tell you. Sound fire at will, bugler."

The double note of the bugle loosed a staccato roll of musket fire that stopped the lancers like a stone wall. A score of horses fell, kicking. The giant Hidalgo wheeled his horse and shouted a single word. The charge of the lancers veered and swung back out of range, leaving the field to the infantry.

Behind rocks and clumps of cholla the Mexicans dug in, pouring balled lead into the blue-gray line drawn across the field. With a jolt of alarm, Standage saw a dozen small brass field pieces being wheeled into position close behind them.

"Sound cease firing," he told Reagan.

Looking to the rear, he saw the Second Texas drawn up in ragged formation. The captain beckoned Lieutenant Barney, and, as the first volley of cannon fire crashed into the lines, they loped back.

Stout met them in the shade of a paloverde. There was blood on his coat from a lance wound on the forearm. Sweat coursed his cheeks. He looked old and weary and his eyes were filled with despair.

"The fight goes against us, Mister Standage," he said huskily. "Had I taken their artillery, Villalobos would be ours. I failed because I was too blind to count the odds." He hesitated a moment, striving against the last vestige of an old pride. Then he said: "The fight is yours. For what they are worth, the dragoons are yours to command."

All cockiness gone, Mr. Barney waited for Standage's reply. Standage thought: *Ten years I have waited for this moment and now it is here there is no satisfaction in it.* He realized that the only vindication he sought was of his methods as a soldier, not of himself as an officer of courage and judgment.

"Our hope lies in the strength of the men," he said. "I do not care how far we must retreat, just so the battle goes according to plan. We must save our powder. If we can draw the lancers into a frontal attack, our fire power will cut them to pieces. For the infantry, we will still have steel."

Stout frowned, pulling at his mustaches. "But if Hidalgo chooses to wear us down, man by man . . . ?" And he looked beyond to where the Americans crouched behind every conceivable shelter, helpless under the bombardment of artillery and the snapping, small teeth of musketry.

"I am gambling," said Standage, "that my own dull infantry tactics will not appeal to him." He returned to his men. "For what they are worth." Standage knew the badly shocked troopers of the Second Texas would be only a liability from here on. Win or lose, the battle rested on the shoulders of the infantry.

He had hardly reached his post when the cannon fell silent. In the next moment the Mexican infantry rose at one impulse and came in a yelling horde across the field.

When the little brown men were too close for a ball to miss its target, Standage let the Texans send their bullets crashing into them. Going to their knees, they fired, primed, drew bead, each flashing salvo hacking bloody gaps in the line. The fury went out of the assault. The attackers struggled forward another dozen yards, and then fell back to the shelter of a shallow draw.

For the first time, Reagan's brown face showed excitement. Caught up by the savage battle urge running like a flame through the troops, he fingered his bugle as though needing only the captain's confirmation before sounding the charge.

What Standage said was: "Sound the retreat." When Reagan stared, he repeated angrily: "Sound retreat, bugler! At this range we shall be cut to tatters, for we have not the powder to return their fire."

Lieutenant Barney, hearing the call, looked across the

battlefield, and his lips formed one word: "Mad!"

Retreat was costly. There were wounded to carry, while the cannon pounded them mercilessly. They dug in again—sweating, cursing, rebellious men who fingered the triggers of their long rifles hungrily.

And always Standage watched the Mexican general as he moved up and down behind his lines. When would he weary of his game of fox and hounds and hurl his lancers in another bloody charge?

Twice, in the hours that followed, he sent his infantry forward in savage assaults. Twice the Americans arrested them. But always they were crowded back. Standage rode among his men, reading cruel exhaustion in their faces. The iron fortitude they had won in long months' of training was deserting them.

Suddenly Lieutenant Barney came at a lope through the smoke and dirt. "They're bringing up their twelve-pounders, sir! The men can't stand much more of this."

Standage said: "I know." He spurred his pony over to a bearded sergeant kneeling beside a boulder. The man's forage cap was off and he had a bloodstained rag twisted about his head. "How many rounds have you left, Sergeant?" he asked.

The soldier let eight balls tumble from his bullet pouch onto his hand. "Eight rounds, sir." Then his mouth made a crooked smile. "And sixteen inches of steel when you call for it!"

Some of the tension in Standage relaxed. The effect of this, the first expression of faith in his leadership, was like warmth of brandy in him.

"You will need both of them," he said to the man. "Steel for the infantry, balled lead for the lances!"

Glancing back, he saw the dragoons drawn up in attack formation, a bloody little band ready to die to redeem its name, but he thought: *Let them fill in where the loss is heaviest. I shall not be the one to send them against the lancers.*

Abruptly he snapped an order at Reagan. The corporal's jaw sagged when he heard it. "Did you say . . . charge, sir?"

"If you prefer," Standage said, "I will sound the call myself. It is a great responsibility to blow such a call."

Reagan wiped the mouthpiece of the bugle with his sleeve, grinning. "It is the one call I could blow with a clear conscience, sir!"

The bugle notes cut through the battle sounds, a bright, clean blade. For a moment the troops, dulled by their losses, showed no reaction. Then they began to stir. Non-commissioned officers turned to confirm what they had heard. When they saw Standage erect in the stirrups, saber raised, a shout went up.

Standage breathed a prayer. "Lord, make them strong, as I have tried to make them!" And he brought the saber down.

With a cry that seemed to hush even the cannon, the troop went out. Mr. Barney and Mr. Pierce, yelling, led their companies. Standage heard the impeccable Mr. Pierce shout: "Meat for your bayonets, men!" Mr. Barney's speech seemed to be a stream of profanity.

The sound of the assault went up to the sky. Muskets roared and bayonets clashed with the noise of giant scimitars being honed. Standage hacked right and left, knowing a hot satisfaction in the feel of bone and flesh under his blade. Fighting like madmen, the Texans strove to pry the enemy out of its stronghold. But there was a dogged savagery to the Mexicans' resistance. They held their ground stubbornly.

From the high ground behind the lines, the cannon poured their shrapnel pointblank into the attackers, tearing the line apart like rotten rags. Under the lash of desperation Standage spurred forward, fighting to silence the murderous field pieces. Behind him, a wedge of fighting men pressed ahead until a bristling wall of bayonets hurled them back.

For the first time, the crushing weight of hopelessness

descended on the captain. He glanced along the battle line and saw that with his men it was the same. Dog-tired, they were falling back.

Then a new sound roused him—a high whooping riding on the thunder of hoofs. Through the battle haze he discerned a column of horsemen sweeping behind the Mexican line. From both sides they came—hard-riding cavalrymen under the red guidon of the Second Texas!

The rifles saw and understood. They were not fighting alone. Stout had brought his ragged band out for another sortie, with death or victory the prize.

Again the lancers came out, fresh, burning for action. But this time they were forced to divide their strength to meet the two-pronged attack of the Americans. On the right, Stout threw his troopers against the Mexicans, riding the vanguard down with saber and pistol. Standage saw the blue-and-gold tide roll over the batteries of six- and twelve-pounders, saw the colonel and a crew of dragoons leap to the ground and hack their way through the cannoneers.

A shout came from the throats of his men as they realized what was happening. The dragoons were turning the cannon on the Mexicans! Lancers and terrified infantry alike, they were swinging the smoking muzzles upon them.

The first shell sliced through the infantry like a scythe, cutting a gory lane before it exploded among the riflemen. Into the gap rushed a spearhead of Texans.

Blast of solid shot tore a hole in the left flank, giving a toe hold for another pry bar of bayonets.

Hidalgo was tasting the same gall he had poured down the throats of the dragoons. Sweating cavalrymen, glutting the cannon with powder and shot, worked bloody slaughter among the horsemen. A host of Mexicans were already down. The rest showed growing signs of panic.

The Second Texas, from the colonel down to the scurviest private, was on the march. Their sabers sang with vengeance as they hacked the painted lances aside. Standage heard their war cries as he led his exultant forces deeper into the sagging line. There was no semblance of orderly retreat. At a dozen spots the Texans had broken through, doubling back to throw rings of steel about the Mexicans.

The guns were roaring incessantly. Against the screaming showers of razor-edged shrapnel not even Hidalgo's reckless border wolves could stand. Knowing that, the Mexican rallied his lances for a final assault. But the war gods were laughing even as he plunged forward. Stout's saber fell, and in the roar and flash of burning powder Hidalgo's last hope of victory was snuffed out. When the smoke cleared, there was no sign of the giant. But under the stampeding hoofs of the lancers' mounts could be seen flashes of the hide of the white stallion.

It was enough for the lancers. Lances stained with the blood of many a border soldier began to fall to the ground in token of surrender.

Stout wheeled to give aid to Captain Standage, but he saw immediately that the infantryman needed no help. Over the Mexican lines fluttered his own blue guidon. Hidalgo's infantry, too, had had enough.

III

Colonel Stout did not forget his promise of that morning: "Supper in Villalobos!"

In a smoky tavern off the plaza, the officers dined hugely on barbecued beef and red Mexican wine. Through the windows came the clamor of roistering troopers, eating and drinking under the chinaberry trees.

Standage was conscious of the glances of Mr. Barney and

Mr. Pierce. The smugness they had brought with them from officers' school had been washed out in the bright blood of battle. Their eyes were respectful and a little awed.

Colonel Stout leaned across the table to refill the captain's glass. "I shall be borrowing your textbooks one day soon," he said casually. "It occurs to me that we might work out some tactical problems now and then to the benefit of us both."

"No textbook in my library could have shown you how to lead your men back from hell today," he said.

"If I had studied your texts," the colonel told him, "I should not have led my men to hell in the first place." He stood up, his glass raised. "A toast, gentlemen . . . not to the man who showed us how to thin our powder with blood and sweat, for every private in Villalobos has toasted him tonight. I give you General Hidalgo . . . for teaching an old fool more humility than he had learned in fifty years!"

Reagan was waiting in the shadows when Standage left to spread his blankets under the trees. "I have a favor to ask, sir," the corporal said with some uncertainty.

Standage waited while he hesitated over his words. Reagan was holding his bugle by the sling. He raised it now and said: "This bugle, sir . . . it isn't really mine, you know. It's Quartermaster property. I was thinking that, if you would report it as lost in battle, I'd be mighty grateful."

"You want it as a souvenir?"

"That's it. The barracks is a great place for talk. Many a yarn I'll be spinning for the recruits about today's bloody business. I was thinking that if I had it for proof, the men would be slower to call me a liar."

"Is it," Standage asked quietly, "the same bugle that blew the charge for Standage, of San Felipe?"

Reagan slung the bugle over his shoulder. "That yarn I have forgotten, sir. But it will be a proud day when I sit on my bunk a-polishing it, and say to the lads . . . 'This is the bugle that blew the charge for Standage, of Villalobos.' "

★ ★ ★ ★ ★

DEVIL'S GRAZE

★ ★ ★ ★ ★

I

Kearny saw her first the day she and her father stopped at Cedar Lodge on their way to the dubious paradise the government had staked out for homesteaders on the San Augustin Plains. They had stayed for lunch before filling their water barrels and moving on. Kearny had sat with them, liking the powerful, graying man who was Gus Stoneman, and feeling the quiet strength of this thoughtful granger.

But over everything else he remembered Fran—the golden sunlight burnishing her hair that was like crystal-clear honey, making her eyes seem darker, her skin dusky-smooth; he remembered how her laughter had been like the *tinkle* of ice in a thawing creek, and how she had given him her hand when they left, smiling into his eyes in simple thanks. And he recalled thinking: *Fifteen years you've told yourself that land and cattle and security are all that matter . . . and now I wonder if any of them do.*

In the two years since, he had watched many nesters come in with their wagons bulging with wives, kids, and the tools a man needed to bludgeon a living from the earth. Scores of them he had provided with a square meal on their way out a year or so later, beaten and discouraged by a land that was never meant for farming. His beef, slow-elked, had fed most of them anyway. He was glad enough to send them on their way.

But through those thorny months the Stonemans had hung on, they and a few other determined homesteaders. They had remained by the grace of Charlie Haight's credit at the general store and Lyle Kearny's inability to catch them butchering his beef. What might have been friendship between Kearny and Gus Stoneman had turned to enmity.

On the streets, in council meetings, on the road, he met and spoke to Fran Stoneman. As ever, he was all hardness and arrogance. It was the front he had always shown around Kingbolt, as much a part of him as his checkered shirt, sweat-stained vest, and Levi's. His blue eyes were like sharp-cut stones in the brown face full of lean angles.

Once she had said to him: "I don't think you like me, Mister Kearny. Do you regret the day you let us fill our water barrels at your well?"

"It isn't you I dislike, Miss Stoneman, or your father. The government sent you out here on a wild-goose chase, and the sooner your father and his friends realize that and go home, the sooner we'll all stop suffering because of a foolish mistake."

But in these meetings Lyle Kearny tried not to let the girl know by so much as the inflection of his voice that she had been in his mind every hour for two years.

She's too young for you, he told himself. *She's only a girl. She's for young bucks like Budd.*

Kearny's younger brother Budd had taken her to socials and meetings, ignoring Lyle's objections and the fact that she was the daughter of the man who led the forces arrayed against them.

In October, the mounting tide of grievances received an impetus that promised to divide the Kingbolt country by one stroke. Gus Stoneman, a councilman by now, proposed that a dam be built on Kearny's land to impound water for irrigation purposes.

Kearny was now ready for war, his patience ended. To be on hand early for the council meeting at which the proposition would be launched or struck from the fall ballot, he left for town the preceding afternoon.

In the red, streaming twilight he splashed through the ford of Hangman's Creek, on his south forty. As he came out of the creek, a flash of white drew his glance up the *bosque* and he rode close to find a white stake driven into the sand. There were surveyor's figures on it that meant nothing to him. But it meant something, that a chain and transit should have been across his land at all.

Farther along he found two more stakes, and then a third, and just before dark he saw smoke in the green piñons beneath a low hummock. Lyle Kearny rode into a small camp at which two men sat at supper.

"Howdy!" hailed one of the men. "Light down and have some chuck."

"I can say what I've got to say without dismounting," Kearny replied coldly. "What are you men doing on my range?"

The man's eyes were confident in a flat-featured, unshaven face. "Government men," he said. "The Agriculture Department's looking for some new Taylor grazing lands. We're running trial lines."

"Not on my land," snapped Kearny. "This is patented. You're invited to take your stakes and get."

"I reckon," said the dish-faced man, "you'll have to take that up with Washington."

Kearny's eyes had that smoky look, his lips that stiffness, that presaged trouble. "Washington never heard of you," he remarked. "You're running lines for irrigation canals. And I'm giving you five minutes to pack and get out."

The men looked at each other. Grinning, the first said: "I'd hate to see you make a mistake you'd regret. Suppose we compromise. You give us another week to finish up and we'll pull out."

Lyle Kearny did not reply but his arm came up in a smooth

arc and a rope sang through the air. A loop settled about the two men before they could scramble out of the way. Kearny took a dally about the horn and gave his pony the spurs.

He dragged the pair down the needle-strewn slope to the *bosque,* snaked them through the willows, and into the shallow stream. He gave the shouting, swearing pair a 100-yard trip upstream through the cold water before he slackened the rope and let them free.

They stood there, two shivering, bruised, and ragged figures in the middle of the stream, staring at him as he coiled his rope.

"I always give a man a chance to be reasonable first," Kearny said. "Then I throw the rules overboard and play the game his way. I'll be riding through here again tomorrow and I'd like to find you boys gone."

At a high trot, he rode on.

Kearny and Budd spent the night at the hotel. In the morning, Budd put on his Stetson and started out while Kearny was still before the mirror with lather snow on his long jaws.

Kearny spoke sharply and Budd turned back, sullenness in his eyes. Budd's strength was in his shoulders; the compactness of them was patterned in his short arms and deep chest. He wore brown whipcord clothes bought with the girls in mind, where his brother was always thinking of horse and rope when he paid his money. He was shorter than Lyle but neither man was one a bully would choose to disturb.

"What's the hurry?" Kearny demanded.

"Going down and have some coffee." Budd stood with one hand on the knob and the other tucked under his belt.

"You couldn't wait another five minutes?" Kearny suggested tartly.

"I could . . . but what's the difference? Might as well get down to the meeting."

With meticulous care, Kearny drew the lather from the long blade of the razor with his thumb. "I reckon we'll go in together," he said. "We'll be facing down that nester outfit practically alone. We've got to look like we're unified even if we aren't."

Budd's gray eyes met his across the room. "I'm meeting Fran at the hall. I'll be setting with her."

"Don't be a damned fool!" Kearny's voice had a vicious thrust. "It'll be kitty-bar-the-door down there this morning. I'm going to tear up the furniture and beat those sun-pecked plow-chasers' ears off if I have to. And I don't want you hanging back because of a girl."

Budd's handsome face grinned, sarcasm in the turn of his lips. "And that's right where the saddle rubs. She's a nice set-up filly, ain't she? Maybeso you'd like to see yourself settin' with her. . . ."

The challenge brought the hot blood to Kearny's face, but he knew that to lose his temper would give the lie to his own denial. He made a short, contemptuous snort. "We've fought over everything else under the sun. Let's not go to war over a girl. That kid! What is she, seventeen . . . eighteen? Twenty, then. I'm thirty-three . . . and I might as well be a hundred, as far as women are concerned. I've been too busy to think of them since I was fifteen years old."

"Too old!" Budd said it with a sly sharpness in his eyes. "When a man gets to thinking he's too old to fall for a woman, it's time to watch out."

Kearny, turning back to the mirror, laid the razor again to his cheek. "You can have her, with my blessing . . . after we whip this thing. If they put those bonds through, we may as well take up homestead claims ourselves."

"They're not asking much. Just enough water to make a crop on."

Again Lyle stopped shaving, and this time he laid down the razor abruptly and faced his brother.

"Let's get this straight . . . whose side are you on?"

"I've tried to stay on the fence where I could decide how things stacked up without getting excited," Budd snapped. "You've badgered me until I've about decided to side the Stoneman crowd. They've got a side, too, you know."

"Yes . . . they want water. And they must build a dam to get it. I'm the hog-greedy range baron who don't let them have it. It never enters their heads, nor yours apparently, that I'll support over half the cost of that dam! Not a man of those grangers pays taxes. Most of the other cattlemen in this county are two-bitters squatting on government forest leases or land they haven't proved up on yet, so they don't pay any taxes. These bull-headed fools have lived so far by slow-elking my steers and hauling water from my tanks. And so help me I'll sell out the Padlock before I'll foot the expense of their irrigation project!" Kearny paused, and his dark eyes were resentful. "Here I am calling it my ranch . . . when it's half yours. It's a natural mistake. I've done all the worrying, all the planning, and most of the work on it since the old man died."

"And all the bossing," said Budd. "You've run it up from a few sections until it takes in a third of the county. You could bring a cow to prime on a handful of corn and a bucket of water. And you don't let me forget it, nor anybody else. You're a big man, Lyle, but not a popular one."

"Do I give a damn for that? It was hardness I needed to hold the ranch against the men who tried to take it away from us, so I was hard. It was sharpness that would take us over the tough spots when beef prices fell, so I was sharp. I hewed mighty close to the line, and I can still do it. You like a pocketful of money, Budd, and you like fancy duds and blooded horses. You aren't going to have those things if we lose out. Just think about that when this thing is dragged out on the floor."

"I like to see a starving man get a plate of beans, too," Budd said, and turned and went stiffly out of the room.

Kearny looked at the closed door and it was like a symbol of all the things he had cut himself off from—the little pleasures, the extravagances, the luxuries. Not through choice. You didn't carry along a piano and a trunk full of fancy clothes when you went to war, and it was war he had been fighting all these years.

He finished shaving and put on his denim jumper. He strapped on an old Colt .45 and let his hand linger on the smooth walnut butt, longingly. The old days were best, after all. You voted with lead, then, and to hell with council meetings.

He was the last man to enter the hall, and the babble of voices died gradually as he went through the room toward a seat by the window. He shook hands curtly with two or three other men, ranchers who stood to lose with him, if the bonds carried. He sat down beside his range foreman, shaggy-browed, uncurried old Steve Jones.

Charlie Haight, who was mayor as well as general store owner, opened the meeting with a clout of a mallet on a clumsy pine table. In the front row of benches sat Gus Stoneman, Jess Riley, and Sheriff Lang. Fran sat with Budd, slender and fresh-looking in a bright print dress; she seemed as cool as a breeze off a green spring meadow, and the gold of her hair was brighter, the color of her eyes even more like that of a blue mountain lake than on that long-gone day at Cedar Lodge.

Charlie Haight rattled some papers and stood up, stiff as old leather, in black store clothes and a boiled collar. He was dressed as if for a funeral, and from the tension in the atmosphere it seemed one might develop. Haight's raw-looking face was redder than usual, his body heavier. Apparently he had profited by the nesters' presence.

"We'll have roll call of the council members first," he said, "and then we'll get down to business. This meeting ain't to vote on the bonds, as some of you seem to think. That's next week. I've got bids here on the equipment and materials we'll need to throw up a dirt dam."

No, this wasn't the regular election, Lyle Kearny thought, but it might as well be. If the councilmen, of which he was one, let the proposition go on the ballot, it would carry as sure as the sun rose, for nesters outnumbered cattlemen three to one.

The "present!" of eleven councilmen came from here and there in the crowd and Haight sat down to put on silver-rimmed glasses and scan the papers. "Looks like the best bid we got is four thousand dollars. That's for graders and lumber and concrete for the spillways. I understand you boys are willing to do all the labor yourselves?"

Gus Stoneman said: "That's right."

"Then," said Charlie Haight, "is there any discussion before we put 'er to a vote?" He looked directly at Kearny as he spoke.

Kearny stood up, hitched at his belt, and let his glance go over the expectant heads below him. Then his sharp voice broke the silence.

"There's just this much discussion from my camp," he said, "and I'm talking to Gus Stoneman. I've put up with your stealing my beef and pasturing your work animals and milk cows on my forest leases. I've paid taxes on school bonds for four schools, though there aren't a dozen tax-paying men here with kids in school. This dam you're prattling of . . . you want to put it on my land, in Rimrock Cañon. You want to float it on a bond issue that I and a few others will pay for. I can't stop you from passing those bonds. I could reason with you, but I know the uselessness of that. So all I can do is to lay down some law of my own and back it up with a threat. There'll be no dam built on my land. There'll be no more of my steers slow-elked.

If I catch any man butchering one of my beeves, I'll kill him. And if one spade is sunk in Rimrock Cañon, there'll be a war in Kingbolt that will make the Tonto Basin feud seem like target practice."

Gus Stoneman was on his feet, his jaw stuck out like a fist. He had his hands tucked under his belt, and his shoulders set well back.

"That kind of talk will bring war as quick as you want it," he said. "There have been beeves stolen . . . sure. But not by me or any of the boys I'm talking for. We've had some plenty lean meals. We've done our best to leave you strictly alone. As soon as we could, we built windmills to irrigate our pastures. But most of them wore out with pumping night and day, so we've had to haul water from your tanks again."

"You bought the parts for them from Haight," answered Kearny. "That was your mistake. Mine pump year in and year out. But I brought in good casings so they'd last."

Haight scowled under his cold glance. Stoneman looked at the merchant, frowning; then remarked: "Anyway, they're worn out. Try to look at this from our standpoint. We came, some of us fifteen hundred miles, to this new homestead tract. We left farms we could exist on for dry-land patches that won't support a jack rabbit. You boast that you're a fightin' man so I reckon you can savvy why we ain't ready to quit. We've proved to ourselves that this soil is rich and deep, but no land will produce without water. But for a comparatively small cost we can dam up Rimrock Cañon and save the winter rains and snow for when we need them."

Kearny said: "At a small cost . . . to you."

"They'd pay if they could," put in Charlie Haight impatiently. "Besides, you're painting it too black when you say they won't pay none of the cost. Most of them will prove up in a couple of years. They'll be paying taxes, then, and the bonds will have twenty years to go,"

"We'll do even better than that, if you'll let us," Stoneman told Lyle. "Why don't you make us an outright loan of four thousand dollars at eight percent, and collect interest on the money instead of paying it out?"

It was the mayor who replied, his syllables short. "That's foolishness. You'd be putting yourselves right in his hands."

"If I lend you any money," said Kearny, "it will be to make a quick trip yonderly."

"Then," said Stoneman, letting his thick, hard bulk into the chair, "I guess we've talked this out. Suppose we put it to a vote."

Charlie Haight raised his hand. "All in favor of putting this bond. . . ."

Lyle Kearny strode, tall and hard-eyed, down the aisle and out of the hall. It was eight to three, no need to cast his vote.

After him there came a quick measure of footfalls and Fran's voice called his name. He stopped, not turning, waiting until she came up with him, her cheeks flushed. Kearny's heart wrenched. Looking at her, feeling the sudden emptiness in his stomach, he knew that nothing could ever take from him this bitter yearning that might have been different.

"Does it have to be like this?" Fran asked him.

"How else can it be? A man's going to resent it when he's being robbed."

"We don't want to do it this way. Why do you make us? We could all work together if you wouldn't fight us every inch of the way."

"If I took a herd of five thousand cattle to Illinois," Kearny said harshly, "would the farmers welcome me into their midst with a brass band?"

Fran's blonde head shook. "The East is crowded. That was why we had to leave. This is different. . . ."

"It's only different because you stand to win by backing me down."

Steve Jones and Budd came out of the hall onto the board-walk. Kearny turned from the girl. To the range boss, he said: "Come along, Steve. We've got business to talk over. You, too, Budd. You can look up your lady friend later."

Over beers in the gloomy saloon, he told them: "I heard from Talbot yesterday. He'll be in town the Second of November to buy steers. That gives us a month to cut out four hundred prime two-year-olds and throw them over on the east forty. You and I will take some boys and work the south sections, Steve. You, Budd, will curry the hills for what you can find between the Lodge and Palo Pinto."

Budd nodded, eyes veiled. Kearny watched his face steadily.

"That's the Rimrock Cañon section," he reminded him. "We've made our brag that they won't build their dam, bonds or no bonds. You'll know what to do if they try to come in."

II

It was nine days later when, with Steve Jones and a tired crew of grimy cowboys, Kearny trailed the big Padlock day herd across the hills east of the Cedar Lodge headquarters. Quick tallow would slab to the chunky bones of the Herefords in the green meadows lying between parallel ridges of the piñon-stippled range.

They found no cattle on the fattening range, other than a few strays. Riding back to headquarters, Lyle stopped on a prominence above the ranch buildings and his glance went far across the valley to the timbered section north and west. He searched for dust sign, for the flash of horns in the gray-green foothills, and the quest turned up nothing.

They rode down the cañon to the ranch, threw the work-worn remuda into the trap, and stalled a wrangling pony with a few forkfuls of hay. Dog-tired, every man was ready to wash up at the trough under the oaks and spend the afternoon smoking in the shade.

Without any word to the rest, Kearny rode into the pasture, cut out a fresh horse, and switched his saddle. He pointed then for Rimrock Cañon.

In the middle of the afternoon he came down off the ridge above the head of the cañon. He switch-backed to the narrow cañon floor, the rough walls shelving away high above him, shadows filling the gorge. Over the rocky streambed, splashed with greens and blues where the water brought out deep mineral coloring in the boulders, an icy rivulet brawled its way toward the valley. That rivulet would grow bolder and stronger, choked with the run-off of winter snows after spring and Old Man Winter had their annual fight. The water would fill a score of small creeks until midsummer; it would raise Kearny's dirt tanks to the brim.

Then his head canted sharply to one side as he caught a far-off *jingle* of sound. Riding on, he came around a sharp in bend the gorge and there stopped his pony with a yank of the reins.

Where the cañon bottled between opposing cliffs of granite, a dozen giant boulders had been rolled from the heights to block the passage. Along the slopes above this point, a crew of grangers worked with mules and graders, bringing loads of earth to pile against the boulders.

In the bottom of the cañon, watching the work, were Fran Stoneman and Jess Riley, Charlie Haight's freight boss. And beside them, on a flat rock, sat Budd.

Lyle Kearny left his pony in a little motte of wolf willows, going slowly down the trail to where the three conversed with their backs to him. He came to within a few feet before Jess Riley heard him and turned his head. Riley gave a start and pivoted, his boots grinding in the gravel, and Budd saw Lyle then and came to his feet. Fran Stoneman looked startled, but defiance, not guilt, was what heightened the flush of her features.

"Comin' along fine, ain't it?" Kearny spoke in the most conversational of tones, nothing in his manner showing the fury that possessed him except the hard ridges of white muscle that crossed his flat brown jaws.

Riley's fingers cramped into big fists. He was a hard-bitten muleskinner with the marks of a score of battles on his face, a tall man constructed, like the wagons he drove, for rugged strength at the sacrifice of beauty. He had a jaw a blacksmith could have shaped a shoe on, a broad nose of which some teamster's boot toe had made havoc. But he knew Kearny's reputation for being handy with his fists, and his manner was apprehensive.

"She's comin' along great," he told Lyle Kearny. "And she's going to keep on coming. So don't get any ideas about starting anything."

Budd was stubbornly defiant. "The bonds went over," he told Lyle. "Everything's being done legally. Don't make a lot of trouble for yourself by trying to stop what's going to be done anyway."

Kearny, ignoring him, asked Jess Riley: "Are you bossing this?"

Riley nodded.

"Then get them out of here," Kearny said. "Get them out before I personally break every nose, black every eye, and crack every rib in camp."

"Wait a minute," Riley interposed. "Maybe we ain't made it plain that we've started something we aim to finish. For your own good. . . ."

Kearny started toward him then, and Jess Riley showed his fear of the rancher's fists by taking a step backwards. But Kearny came on, the bony structure of his face in hard relief, his jaw set. Panic dictated a move to the muleskinner that common sense could have told him to check.

He yanked his gun as though to hold the other man at bay.

Fran Stoneman's cry rose sharply. Along the steep cañon sides workmen straightened and watched.

Kearny was upon Jess Riley, then, in a swift, vicious drive. He had the freighter's wrist in his grip before the Colt came level and the .45 spat flame and lead into the ground between his feet. He put a twisting pressure onto the wrist that made Riley's eyes wince and caused the gun to drop. Then Kearny slugged him across the jaw savagely.

Jess Riley went back into the rock. His face was the color of cold tallow, with two rivulets of blood starting from his nose. But the pain did something for that watered courage of his; he came back swinging like a windmill, teeth set and the breath whistling through them.

Lyle was aware of grangers pouring down the slope but he was more watchful of Riley's frantic swings. He ducked one, warded off a couple with elbows and shoulders, and took a grazing punch on the cheek bone that rattled his teeth.

For an instant the teamster slowed, catching breath. His man measured, Kearny went to work. One short, searching punch buried Riley's belt buckle in his stomach. As Riley doubled with a gasp, Kearny hit him on the ear with a powerful, looping blow. Riley went to his knees, and the cowman hauled him up by the shirtfront and pulled a downraking fist across his nose. Then he threw a punch that appeared leisurely, but rocked Jess Riley's head on his grotesquely rubbery neck. Riley reeled into the boulder, bounced off it, and went face down in the trail.

The grangers, who had come on the double-quick, were still straggling in. Lyle bent to pick up the muleskinner's Colt, so matter-of-factly that they seemed not to notice this move until he straightened with Riley's gun in his left hand and his own in his right. There was a sudden, startled shifting as they realized he had the drop on them.

"What they say about good Injuns applies to grangers, too," he said. "Don't force me to make good grangers out of any of you. You've done all the dam building you're going to do. If you've got horses, find 'em and ride. Otherwise, start walking."

Budd stood, angry-eyed, beside Fran, holding her hand. "You'd think these men were yellow curs if they didn't fight back," he said. "And they're going to. They'll be back, primed for war. What happens will be on your head."

"We'll see about that when the time comes," said Kearny. His face, his eyes looked old and hard. "We've played our string out, Budd," he said. "You've got a right to your own opinions but I'm not going to see the Padlock ruined because of them. I'll meet you at Sam Caine's tomorrow. We'll split the land and cattle. Then, if you want to put your land into corn and chili, you can do it. But as long as I can buy shells, the Padlock is going to be no-man's land for nesters."

Lyle Kearny was in Kingbolt early. He spent the morning with lawyer Sam Caine, seeing the Padlock divided as impartially as possible. For him, it was like having an arm amputated. He had given fifteen hard, bitter years to holding the ranch together, adding a section here and a section there, weeding out the bad blood and importing good herd stock. Now it was akin to starting over.

At noon Budd arrived. They sat at opposite corners of the lawyer's desk and the dry, sour-faced little man shoved each a copy of the deeds.

"I'm giving you the lodge," Kearny told Budd. "You'll be taking a wife someday and she'll want better than a mud shack to set up housekeeping in. I'll make out at the Cold Springs line camp for a spell."

Budd scratched his name at the bottom of a paper. When he looked up at his brother, his mouth had a humorless quirk.

"I'll be puttin' it to use right soon," he said. "Fran and I are getting married next Sunday. I'd like to have you best man me, if you can take time off from the ranch for the wedding."

Kearny managed to say, without changing his voice, or his expression: "Congratulations. But I won't be down. Maybeso Jess Riley will do the honors."

Afterwards, he stood on the walk in the warm fall sunlight, but the warmth did not touch his flesh. Everything he had fought for, everything he had won, turned to ashes in his grasp when he thought of the one thing he had wanted that he could not win, that now he could never own.

He had two whiskies at the saloon. When he came out, he saw three of Haight's wagons taking on earth-moving equipment before the general store. Haight was bustling about with loud advice to the swampers and Gus Stoneman stood on the walk with his fists on his hips. Haight looked across the street to see Lyle Kearny watching; he spoke to Stoneman, and the two of them crossed.

The merchant pulled a folded paper from his pocket and shoved it at Kearny. His florid face was hostile, his neck stiff. The rancher glanced down at the document, and Haight snapped: "It's a cease-and-desist. If you pull your iron on any of the boys now you'll be getting striped sunlight for the next few months. We've got the court's signature on that paper and Sheriff Lang's guns to back it up."

Kearny looked beyond them, watching four swampers hoist a fresno to the bed of a wagon. Then he looked at Gus Stoneman, and tucked the paper, folded, in his shirt pocket. If he were surprised or angry, he failed to show it.

"All right," he said. "If that's how it is, there's no use butting my head against the wall. From the way you're throwing credit around, you seem to think the plow's here to stay, Haight. You always raised hell if I asked for credit on a load of salt lick."

Stoneman's sober gray eyes kept watching the cowman. His manner and his voice were guarded. "He knows we can pay, now that we're going to have water. I hope you aren't bluffing about not intending to make trouble. I'd like to be good neighbors with you, Kearny. There's no reason why we can't get along."

Kearny slowly shook his head. "None at all. I expect we'll end up by being right neighborly. By the way, Haight . . . can you send a wagonload of grub to my Rimrock Cañon line camp tomorrow?"

Haight frowned. "What do you want with grub up there?"

Kearny shook golden flakes of tobacco onto a wheat-straw shuck. "I'm sending the boys up with a wagon full of picks and shovels. I figured I might throw up a little diversion dam about two miles above yours. That would push the water down Silvertip Creek. Thought I might put in a few acres of spuds and corn and maybe raise some hogs on the side. This plow shoving's sure the coming thing! See you around, boys."

Gus Stoneman and Charlie Haight were still standing there when he rode out.

For five days Lyle Kearny buried himself in the vast job of getting a diversion dam started near the head of Rimrock Cañon where a dozen small feeder cañons poured their spring floods into the deeper gorge. A raise of thirty feet would throw the stream into Silvertip Cañon, which generally ran dry by the 1st of July.

In part it was bluff, but back of his plan was an iron determination to see it through if he were forced to. It might cost him $1,000 before he was through, but there was no way under heaven that they could stop him without making war, and that would put the grangers back on the shady side of the fence where he wanted them.

There was grumbling and discontent among the cowpunchers. Ordinarily they avoided a shovel as they would have a sand rattler. But Lyle did not crowd them, and on Sunday, the day of Fran's wedding, he let the whole outfit go to town.

He sat around camp for two hours, smoking, working a little, trying to steer his mind from the subject of the wedding. But Fran's face was before him, in the smoke of his cigarette, in the flash and swirl of the creek, in his every thought.

It seemed to pile up on him, this desperation, and finally he knew he could not stand the arching silence of the camp any longer. He had a sudden yen for whiskey, too, and at length he did the logical thing and hit for Kingbolt.

He took a short cut to town, angling across the hills on an old cow trail. Near the rocky spine of a ridge he noticed a flash of white in the underbrush. Riding closer, he discovered another of those white stakes he had found the surveyors driving on his south forty.

Angrily he dropped his rope over it and tore it up, wishing he could have caught the men when they sank it. Three more he found on the trail, and all of them he ripped up and threw deep into the buckbrush. He took a rough sighting across the points where they had been driven and discovered they approximated a curve along the side of the cañon. This, then, proved they were not surveying for any government tract, or the line would have been relatively straight. On the other hand, they would not be planning to run their canals uphill in this fashion.

But heavier thoughts had pushed this to the back of his mind by the time he reached Kingbolt well after noon. There was little activity on the streets. Most of the grangers and a lot of cattlemen were out at Gus Stoneman's place to help chivaree the newlyweds.

He entered the saloon and asked for rye and the bartender made a mark on the bar bottle and set it out with a glass. Lyle was pouring his second drink when he heard a man in the rear begin to sing. The song was an alcoholic rendition of the wedding march. The voice—Kearny went cold, hearing it—was Budd's.

Two other voices blended with Budd's, and then laughter swelled over the singing and the song ended. Kearny saw Budd, tousle-headed and bleary-eyed, pound the table with his glass. "Baldy! Three more o' the same!"

Then Budd saw Lyle crossing the room toward him. Charlie Haight and Jess Riley turned to watch him advance, Riley coming to his feet clumsily, this time making no motion to draw his gun. His face was bruised and marked with ugly cuts.

Kearny stood above the table, a strange mix of emotions on his face. He said: "I thought the wedding was for two o'clock. It's one-thirty now."

Budd cocked his head on one side, slack lips grinning. "Little joke on the bride," he said. "Ain't going to be no wedding."

Something went through Lyle Kearny like a cold blade. "You're drunk," he snapped.

Budd pulled a gold wedding band from his vest pocket and let it ring down on the table. "If she wants this, she'll have to come and coax me," he bragged. "The Kearnys are much sought-after *hombres*. Can't be too careful with strange girls."

Kearny looked at Charlie Haight. "This smells like your dirty fingers have been in it," he remarked. "Get on your feet, Budd. We're going to a wedding."

Budd knocked Lyle's hand from his shoulder. The alcohol sharpened his resentment.

"You take the damn' ring," he said. "Maybeso she'll marry you before she knows what she's getting."

Kearny's hand slapped him across the mouth. "Get up! You

aren't going to stand up that kid before all Kingbolt. I don't know what makes you think you can pull a trick like this and rate any higher than a coyote, but, if Fran wants you, you're going."

Budd threw the chair back and came up on his feet swinging. A fist hit Lyle on the ear. He rolled with the blow and came back to seize him by the shoulder.

"You crazy fool!" His voice was sharp with the urge to drive some sense into Budd before it had gone too far. "Can't you savvy that you're humiliating yourself as well as Fran? This is something you'll be sorry for all your life."

Then Budd's fist stabbed into his belly and his words ended in a grunt. The cowpuncher sent a second flailing punch at his head, and Lyle ducked and let the fist whistle by. He took one deep breath and went to work. This was a task that must be done and he was minded to make a thorough job of it.

His first blow sent Budd reeling back through the tables. Budd recovered and came charging back. Kearny met him with a jab in the face. Budd swore and wiped at the flood of scarlet that burst from his nose. He aimed a haymaker at Lyle's jaw, but it was a slow, looping swing that the taller man easily avoided. Lyle hammered two hard rights into his brother's head, pumped a fist into his stomach to double him up. Then he brought him up on his toes with a savage uppercut. The strength went out of Budd. But for Kearny's hands, catching him under the arms, he would have fallen. Lyle let him down in a chair.

He said nothing to Haight and Riley. He rubbed his bleeding, skinned knuckles against a palm, looked down upon Budd a moment, and went out.

It was 3:00 p.m. when Kearny reached the Stoneman farm. A score of wagons clustered among the small buildings, a few nester kids climbing about them; two lean-looking hounds regarded him from the mud stoop as he dismounted. Beyond the raw, red adobe shacks the fields lay under the blue sky—a neat herringbone pattern with other farms to be seen in the distance against the foothills, their crops laid by in the fervent hope of timely rains.

It was strangely quiet for a wedding celebration. Kearny could hear a murmur of conversation inside the house, with an occasional, awkward laugh rising above it. He was on the point of knocking when Gus Stoneman came onto the porch.

Seeing Lyle, Stoneman gave a start. He was red-faced and looked wrung-out with anxiety; he had a big red bandanna handkerchief to his brow, sopping at the perspiration. He lowered the handkerchief, his deep-set eyes staring at the cowman.

He said: "Where's Budd?"

"Budd's been hurt," Kearny said. "He can't make it."

Stoneman's lips became white. "Damn you for the mangiest wolf that ever walked on two legs," he breathed. "What have you done to him?"

"Nothing," Kearny snapped. "He . . . his horse kicked him. He may be laid up several days."

Stoneman's glance went to the other's skinned knuckles, and he remarked dryly: "Did you have to beat the horse off with your bare fists?"

Then Fran was in the door, looking like the dream Kearny had had of her a hundred times, her golden hair, neatly braided, her white gown making her look taller, more slender; only in her eyes did a difference lie, for they were dark and troubled.

"Let me talk to Mister Kearny alone, Dad," she said, and Stoneman looked at her a scowling instant, and then grunted something and went inside.

"You didn't have to do this to save my feelings," Fran said. "I know why he didn't come."

For once the words did not come to his tongue. He was silent, feeling his awkwardness in every bone.

"Don't think too harshly of him," he said, finally. "He was . . . celebrating too heavy, I reckon."

She shook her head. "He wasn't celebrating. I think more of him because he didn't come than if he had. I had to tell him last night why I was marrying him. I like Budd, a lot, but I don't love him. I thought that, if we were married, it might stop things from developing into open war. I know we could be happy, but I had to tell him that my love could never be all his, because . . . part of it belonged to someone else."

Lyle looked at her, the question in his eyes.

"And I'm not going to explain it," she told him. "Thank you for trying to help me." She was gone then, and he was alone, with the hounds sniffing at his boots and an emptiness in his stomach.

III

Kearny's mind flashed to that brief conversation often in the week that followed. And while the little dirt dam rose a foot or two each day, he kept wishing there were a way to stop it. But he couldn't, without cutting the last artery that kept his own cattleman's way of life alive.

He kept guards posted night and day. The grangers had temporarily stopped work, but they were down there, waiting, rifles across their knees and a stifled, desperate mood pervaded the whole camp. They seemed to be waiting some sign, some signal.

Kearny did not hear of Budd until one day when Steve rode in from Kingbolt with a couple of pack horses loaded with food.

"Budd's taking this cracked weddin' bell proposition pretty hard, ain't he?" the grizzled range boss remarked.

"I don't know," said Lyle. "Is he?"

"He was in the Gold Dollar with Jess Riley this morning, drunker'n a hoot owl. Baldy says he ain't been sober in a week."

"Every man to his own pleasures," Lyle remarked, but the news worried him.

Steve regarded him thoughtfully, shrugged then, and commenced unloading the pack animals.

"Seen some more of them stakes," he said presently. "Whole line of 'em running clean across Dutchman's Peak."

"Then they must be new ones. I was past there the other day and there weren't any."

Kearny kept thinking about that and a short time later he saddled his horse and rode toward Dutchman's Peak. He located the stakes and, coming out on a windy, bald ridge, he looked long and steadily across the hills until he picked up two shapes on a far slope, a transit chain for a moment flashing in the sun.

Still Kearny sat there, searching until finally he saw what he was looking for. He picked his way carefully down the slope, working along a ravine in which a small rivulet sparkled. Where a small, cleared bench overlooked the stream, he reined down, staring with hard eyes at a duplicate of the camp he had broken up over two weeks ago. Evidently these men were drawing good pay to hang on after the working over he had given them.

He found a pair of saddlebags under a roll of blankets in the tent. He opened one and shook out a quantity of papers. There were pages of surveyors' data and a few letters, which he began to open. The first was a letter of credit made out to Sam Elkins and Ben Loftus, in the amount of $2,000.

Lyle Kearny looked a long time at the letterhead and at the signature. A lot of odd bits of information he had puzzled over fell into place like coins rattling into slots: the meaning of the stakes; Charlie Haight's place in the scheme; Haight's willingness to carry the grangers' credit when he knew it was a bad risk. The engraved letterhead carried the title, *Great Western Railroad Company*; the signature was that of the vice president.

Kearny put this letter and all the rest back in the saddlebag, slung it across the saddle, and rode back across the stream and into the hills. Not long before he reached the granger camp in Rimrock Cañon he heard what he thought was a gunshot, a sharp explosion followed by noisier echoes that poured down the cañon.

Kearny put his horse to a lope.

When he gained the site of the dam, it was deserted. He sat his horse on the little mound of earth the grangers had raised, scanning the silent camp; there was a coldness along his spine, as he recalled the gunshot. Along the fringes of the creek the mud was chopped by hoofs and the ground beyond was still dark with water that had splashed when horses plunged through.

Then something moved, off in the brush. Kearny's hand flashed to his gun. Fran Stoneman's voice called sharply: "Lyle! It's Fran. Thank God they missed you!"

Kearny left his horse to stride into the brush. There he found the girl standing beside a man who lay on a blanket, his head wrapped with a blood-sopped bandage. She gripped his arm and he saw that her eyes were full of fear.

"Oh, Lyle," she said, "why did it have to come to this? I prayed that it wouldn't. . . ."

"What's happened, Fran? Who's that?"

"Mort Williams. He's coming out of it now. It was just a scalp wound. But he might as well be dead for all that one bullet has caused."

Kearny's lips were dry, his eyes searching her face. "Who shot him?"

"Budd! Mort was standing beside the creek, rolling a cigarette. We heard a bullet hit a rock, and then another shot came and Mort dropped. We saw Budd dodge behind a rock, and then we heard his horse loping up the cañon. Dad and Charlie Haight and the men have gone up to wipe out every man in your camp."

"I didn't send Budd." Kearny's voice, his features, were heavy. "Charlie Haight sent him. I was blind not to understand it all until now. And now it will be like stopping an avalanche bare-handed. But I've got to try."

Just for a moment, before he left, he held her by the arms.

"I'm not sure that I understood you, that day when I came out to tell you Budd wouldn't be coming. But if you meant what I've hoped, it may not be too late for me to make amends. I want you to believe that I haven't intended to hurt anyone . . . only to protect myself. I've fought men all my life, Fran, to save the Padlock. I thought this was something else I had to fight, but if it's not too late, I know that cattlemen and grangers can live together in Kingbolt and help each other. Does that make any difference to you?"

She said—"Yes."—so softly the word hardly passed her lips, but the answer was in her eyes.

For a moment hatred and strife seemed a long way from them, for Kearny had her in his arms and his whole being felt that yearning he had fought against so long; it was like the sharpest pain, and yet it was satisfying and sweet.

But it could last only a moment. He left her and ran back to his horse, knowing he might never taste the sweetness of such a moment again.

Long before he reached his camp he heard the staccato voice of rifle fire. Kearny pushed his pony faster along the trail that led to a ridge above the dam. Through the trees, now, he had an oc-casional glimpse of gunsmoke far below. He came around a bend to where a flat rock leaned outward from the trail, over

103

the cañon. And here he saw Budd lying on his stomach with a rifle at his shoulder.

Budd heard him. He twisted about, swinging the rifle. Recognizing Lyle, he let the gun come down. His face was pasty gray. He stood up, staring at his brother with something like appeal.

"You fool, Budd!" Kearny said. "Why did you do it?"

"Lyle, so help me, I didn't touch him! I shot to miss him three feet. And I did! Then someone else fired and Williams dropped. . . ."

"Why did you try it in the first place?"

"Haight ribbed me up to it." Budd's jaw was hard, creased with sinews under the brown skin. "I've been half drunk ever since that day in the saloon. Haight got me to thinking Gus Stoneman made Fran change her mind. He told me I could put him in a hole by throwing a scare into his men and making them quit. Then Stoneman would be finished. But I didn't intend to hit anybody!"

Kearny was silent. "I'm sorry about the girl, Budd. That day in town I didn't know how it was. . . ."

"Then you were the only one in Kingbolt who didn't. But that's past. A man can get over a girl. But how about this?"

"Where was Haight while you were bushwhacking them?" Kearny asked abruptly.

"Somewhere down in the camp." Budd suddenly saw his meaning, and his eyes widened. "You don't reckon . . . ?"

"I reckon Haight used you for a fall guy. But his shot was as bad as yours . . . he missed, almost. I reckon he's used the whole town for his chessboard, and we've been the pieces he pushed around."

"What do you mean?" Budd demanded.

Lyle swung down, rifle under his arm. He pulled six shells from his cartridge belt and weighed them in his hand.

"I'm going down and explain it to the whole outfit. I'm going to flush Charlie Haight and Jess Riley out like the polecats they are. I've got no more quarrel with Gus Stoneman, Budd . . . nor with you. Like to go down with me?"

Budd reached for his hand and their grip was short and hard. "I'd like to," he said. "Seems like it's been a long time since we sided each other in a scrape."

"We've both learned something," said Lyle. He slung the saddlebags over his shoulder and started down the slope.

He could see that the forces were ranged in two broken lines; his own men along the west slope of the cañon among the rocks and screening brush, Stoneman's across from them. He and Budd walked up the cañon so that they could approach to the very center of the field without being seen, by keeping behind the dam.

Kearny's shout cut through the salvo.

"Steve! Hold your fire. Stoneman, will you listen to me?"

The firing ended, and Lyle and Budd stood there in clean relief atop the dam. "Say it quick!" Stoneman called. "Are you quitting?"

"I haven't started. I was away when this happened. Budd fired at Williams, but he did so without my knowledge. I swear that."

"You swapping his neck for your own?"

"You still don't know me." Kearny sighed. "Budd didn't hit the man, didn't even try to. Haight did it. He ribbed my brother up to trying to throw a scare into you, so that he'd have him as a cat's-paw for his own attempt to start a war."

From an embrasure of rocks some distance above, Haight shouted: "You lying cull! Hit for a rock, Kearny, or I'll drop you where you stand."

"Shut up!" Gus Stoneman barked. "I'm interested, Kearny. What else?"

105

Now Kearny had spotted the locations of Stoneman, Haight, and Riley; he slung the saddlebags into the rocks where the granger boss lay bushed up.

"Look at the papers in that bag. I took them from two *hombres* who've been running surveying lines on my range. I thought they were surveying for irrigation canals, but it doesn't seem like the Great Western would pay for that job, does it?"

He heard paper rustling. Presently he went on: "I'll tell you what it means, if you're slow to catch on, like I was. Haight's been backing you all the time because he wanted to keep you in his debt. Where did he get the thousands it took? From the railroad outfit. They're obviously planning a line through here, and he's been acting as advance man to see that the right of way costs them nothing. He rigged you with inferior well equipment that would only put you further in the hole. He's got you in so deep now you'd probably be years paying him off . . . providing you haven't signed call loans, which, of course, means you get the axe when he chooses to swing it. Do you savvy what it was all leading to? War between us . . . to wreck us both and leave the range clear!"

There was a silence that terminated when Stoneman called. "What about it, Haight? These papers look like the real thing."

Haight's shot broke through his voice, one clean, sharp clap of rifle sound, one of the slugs clipping Kearny across the ribs. He lay a moment, breathing hard, crouching behind a rock. Haight had chosen his position well. He could back out that nest of boulders without a bullet touching him, to storm his ambuscade would mean grave risk.

In the echoing quiet he heard spurs scraping across stone. He raised his rifle quickly, pulled a bead on the narrow slot through which Charlie Haight had shot at him. He released a slug that caromed through the embrasure and brought a howl of pain. While surprise was still in his favor, he sprang across the rock

106

and plunged up the slope.

A face appeared again at the slot, eye squinting over gunsight. Budd fired a quick shot that drove the man back with the shell unexploded. Kearny won the nest of boulders and scrambled to the top. He looked down into the bore of Charlie Haight's Winchester, into Haight's fat red face that was twisted with fear. Blood was streaming from a cut over his eye.

Their gun bores were not ten feet apart, yet, when the merchant fired, the bullet grooved along the walnut stock of Lyle Kearny's .30-30 and went past his ear with a clap of thunder. Kearny was conscious of Budd on the slope above him, shouting something he could not understand. In the next instant he felt the rifle jar his shoulder, and he saw Charlie Haight's face turn to a blood-spattered mask of horror. Haight sat down heavily, leaned back against the boulder, and remained erect with his head slowly lolling forward on his breast.

Kearny did not hear Budd's gun, but when he looked up, Jess Riley was down, spraddled out on his face a short distance beyond the rocks.

He started to turn back, and that was when he realized his wound had taken more out of him than he had realized. Giddily he stumbled, reaching for something to hold onto. Out of the shadows swirling about him came a strong arm to steady him, and Gus Stoneman's voice spoke huskily.

"Easy, cowboy. One of them rattlesnakes must've hit you when you cleaned out the nest."

"They've been poisoning us all," Kearny said. "Filling us with cussedness and vinegar. But what happens from now on will be on our own heads. We've got a problem to lick, and we'll do it without guns."

"There won't be any problem," Stoneman replied, "if we can have that dam."

"You can have it," Kearny said, "and my blessing goes with

it." His vision was clearing and he grinned up at Gus. "Shucks, I'm not hunting any trouble with my father-in-law."

"So you've finally found that out, too," Stoneman remarked. "I've known how Fran felt ever since the day we stopped at Cedar Lodge. If your kids are as slow-witted as you are, Kearny, they'll be in the second grade till they're tripping over their whiskers."

★ ★ ★ ★ ★

HOP YARD WIDOW

★ ★ ★ ★ ★

Darius Peck came down the Six-Mile Valley road in a bright blue turnout with yellow wheels. The green billows of the hop country swelled under the buggy as he drove along. He had just come from the high desert east of the mountains, and his body nourished itself on the moist autumn air of the coastal valley. Spring branches flowed toward the river, blackberry and currant bushes choking them; dark lines of alders criss-crossed the undulating evenness of the farms. It was a green-smelling country, a fertile country. The soil was like a middle-aged woman yearning for a child.

It was a golden year in the hop yards. Hops were bringing 30¢ a pound at the drier; farmers were turning the pages of catalogs, already spending their fortunes. The heavy smoke of the driers, immense shingled buildings topped with blind belfries, tanged the air. Up and down the deep green arbors moved corps of men, women, and children, stripping yellow-green hops into baskets.

A man, standing by a weighing stand at one of the yards, stepped into the road. "Right here, friend! Free camp wood, straw for bedding, feed for your horse. Cent and a half a pound."

"I don't pick," Darius said.

"What do you mean, you don't pick? Everybody picks. The boss' wife and kids are picking. What makes you too good to pick?"

Peck smiled, understanding the foreman's anxiety to get every

111

hop stripped from the vines before rain should sweep across the coastal range and ruin the crop. "I don't pick, but I'll fix that drier of yours. I spotted it smoking from the ridge."

The foreman hesitated, balancing between his duty to turn a talented stray over to his employer and his desire to get one more hand into the field. "All right. Tell Sizemore I sent you, though."

Peck drove through the workers' camp among the alders. Wagons, tents, and blanket lean-tos thronged the bare ground. There was a big commissary where the hop farmer sold food and work clothing. Somewhere a young woman was laughing, and two boys were tussling under the arbors. The workers didn't take it too seriously, stopping frequently to laugh and talk, yet knowing they would weigh out that night at $3 to $5. They were the same people Peck had seen from time to time in the apple valleys under Mount Hood, in the prune orchards of Sacramento. Not bad people, not good. Pickers.

Sizemore, the farmer, was at the drier. The drier was laid, but carts of pale green hops stood waiting to be unloaded. He was evidently far behind in his drying.

"My name is Peck," Darius said. "Your foreman sent me over. Having trouble with the drier, eh?"

"Drier! It's a damned smokehouse! Look at that!" The farmer was gray and florid and overly fat, with a mustache like a German bandmaster. He was limp with sweat. The drier, resembling a waterfront lodging-house in its tall, plain lines, oozed smoke from every shingle.

"New one, eh?"

"I'd trade seven like it for the old one! You see three thousand dollars' worth of hops waiting to be rained on here, and my own crop still in the field. And this everlastingly damned tower of hard luck chooses to choke up!"

"I can fix it," Peck said.

Sizemore skimmed sweat from his red forehead with a finger. He squinted one eye, saw competence in the other's bearing, and said: "A hundred dollars if you can make it draw."

Peck stripped off his coat, put his horse in the shade, and opened the tool chest in the back of the wagon. He selected a level and pursed his lips over a chamois roll of tools. Men were gathering to watch him, and one shook his head to indicate that it could not be done. Peck smiled; anything could be done. He had never fixed a drier before, never so much as fussed with one. But he was an artist among tinkerers. Not exactly a tinker, however. Call him a rebuilder. Let other men build; when the things they built got out of whack, Darius Peck would rebuild them.

It was a reasonably profitable trade, considering, but once in a while he glimpsed on the crest called Forty a man much like himself, but with less bounce, rambling along in a buggy looking for odd jobs. The lack of future in his work worried him.

But it had never really bothered him until the day he met the Widow Firkus. And the day he fixed Sizemore's drier was the day he met the widow.

Inside the drier it was unbearably hot, aswirl with choking sulphur fumes. Hops were piled deep on the floor. Heat rose from the big sheet-metal flue doubling back and forth under the racks. Smoke escaped from every joint of it. It percolated up through the hops, flavoring them, spoiling them. Peck got down to a flue just long enough to lay the level. It scaled in degrees, and he blinked away the tears drawn by heat and fumes long enough to read it.

He went out, his shirt clinging to him like a porous plaster. Sizemore's eyes tried to read his face as he gazed aloft at the open cupola. "Smoke," said Peck, "has to rise. It can't be piped level. There are nearly level spots in your flue."

"I know. I thought I could carry more racks that way. I've got a special dingus on top to catch the wind."

"Well, it isn't catching it."

"But if I stop to tear everything out and relay the flues, the season will be over. The other driers will get all the hops!"

Peck stopped to fill his pipe. He liked drama. "Get me two jacks. She'll be drawing in an hour."

With the jacks at two corners of the drier, they began to turn the screws. The building slowly acquired a list. As it tilted, it seemed to smoke somewhat less. Peck was changing the pitch of the flues at one stroke. It was at this point that a buggy swept into the yard and a young woman stopped a team of handsome dapple grays beside the drier.

She was in her middle twenties, supple and copper-haired and pretty, and Peck stopped working, to stare. The close-fitting bottle-green gown she wore picked up the sheen of her hair and made her fine skin look like skimmed cream. But there were spots of angry color in her cheeks.

"Mister Sizemore!" she said.

Sizemore looked like a big guilty St. Bernard with paws dirty from burying a stolen bone. "What is it, Missus Firkus?"

"You know very well what it is. You've been stealing my pickers again!" She gave the side rail a lash with the rein ends.

"Ma'am, I can't help it if they quit your yard to work in mine. I pay them the same."

"Then why do they quit?" the woman challenged.

Sizemore roused to a degree of temper himself. "Maybe they don't like being robbed in your commissary, ma'am."

"Robbed! I don't give merchandise away, as you do, but my prices are fair. I simply won't cater to pickers as though they were the salt of the earth. Free wood! Brick fireplaces!"

"At this time of year," Sizemore remarked softly, "they are the salt of the earth."

The young woman's eyes, gray as sage, found Peck, standing

there staring at her. He was thinking that she was the prettiest woman he had ever seen, but he wasn't sure she was as angry as she pretended to be.

"Are you one of my men?" she demanded.

He smiled at her. He was a tall, well-built man, tanned and dark-haired, and wearing a well-trimmed mustache. "If I had a mandolin and a straw hat," he said, "I might have a try at being one."

The men listening chuckled. She tipped her chin, but faltered. Then she sat down again. "If those pickers aren't back tonight," she said, "I'll sue for any loss I sustain."

A strange sense of alarm roused Darius. "Where is your ranch?" he asked quickly. "I might stop for a few days, since you're in need of pickers."

She sniffed. "Don't bother. Mister Sizemore probably appreciates your sense of humor more than I ever could."

She shook up the reins.

"Hellcat!" Sizemore panted. "That widder makes more trouble than rain, the red spider, and the Democrats put together. Her husband was a good man, but she's bound we're all out to rob her. Women," he said, "have no business trying to run a ranch. They haven't got the . . . the intellect for it."

"How long has she been a widow?"

"Three years. I wish to God she'd marry and have six kids. It might quiet her down. Priscilla Firkus. . . . Believe me, mister, she speaks for herself."

Peck finished the work; they stood back and watched the heavy pack of gray smoke bulge from the blind belfry at the top of the drier, instead of seeping out all the cracks. Sizemore said: "Mister, you've done it." He paid him on the spot.

All the way down the valley road, Peck had to argue and reason to keep from being shanghaied into the fields. Some of the field bosses were downright unsociable, implying that a man who wouldn't pick was running away from the law, or criminally lazy. Peck made the shaft horse rear over the more insistent, and drove on. The last man he talked to, up where the valley crumpled into the hills and the dog-fennel berry vines of the hillsides made raids into the hopyard, stood in the middle of the road with his hands on his hips, defying him not to pick.

"There ain't anybody past here but the Widow Firkus," he said. "You ain't meaning to work for her?"

"Any reason I shouldn't?"

"Man, you're crazy! She'll cheat you on the scales and rob you in the commissary. And she's got a tinhorn gambler circulating around to pick up anything she misses legitimate."

Peck said: "I can take care of myself." He let the horse walk right up on the foreman. The man jumped back.

Soon it grew dark. Peck drove along until a lantern began to swing at the side of the road, and a big stony-faced man wearing overalls and a collar-band shirt but no collar took hold of the headstall of his horse.

"Here you are," he said; "cent and a half a pound. But you'll pay your own wood and feed bills."

"What if I won't pay them?"

"Then you can go to hell."

Peck's glance narrowed. The approach was in reverse. The go-to-hell line should come after the howdying and civilizing had failed. "All right," he said. "Where shall I camp?"

"Anywhere you like. Get your hay at the barn and your food at the store."

Peck camped, setting up his tiny tent at the back of the wagon. He fed the sorrel and went over him carefully with comb and dandy brush. Then he walked over to the store. It was a sprawling camp; these folks were not much for putting garbage in boxes and keeping washtubs and such out of the way. But they were enjoying themselves, singing and playing, dancing among the trees, and filling the damp valley night with the scent of their cooking and tobacco.

At the store, he bought eggs, milk, meat, and potatoes. He went out onto the porch, intending to yarn a bit with some of the loafers on the steps. Then he saw Priscilla Firkus hurrying toward them. She was holding up the long skirt of her gown. She spoke to them collectively.

"Has anyone seen Mister Bushong?"

"Seen him taking a cart to the drier a while ago," someone said.

"Pshaw!" She stood, undecided.

"Something I can do?" Peck asked.

She recognized him at once. "No." Then: "Well . . . can you make keys?"

Peck descended the steps, caught his groceries under one arm, and put a hand under her elbow to guide her. "We'll pick up my tools at the wagon. I opened the bank vault in Baker last summer when the mechanism failed."

She didn't like being squired that way, but sounded relieved. "I hate having so much money on hand, with so many people around. I've lost the key to the safe, and some of the pickers haven't been paid yet. They'd die before they waited overnight."

The safe was a small wooden one with a painting on the door. Most farmers owned a safe, because of the necessity of having cash on hand to pay the pickers, and for safekeeping the money they received at the driers. Most of them did not own a drier, and merely sold outright.

Peck smoked a blank key and worked it back and forth in the lock. The safe was in a corner of the large old-fashioned living room. The room was cluttered with furniture, gloomy steel-pen pictures, and a reed organ, but seemed somehow to lack life. Smells, he decided, were what it wanted: pipe tobacco and the leathery odors of a working man had not been in this house in much too long. It was as lonesome as the left-hand seat of his wagon.

He filed and tested and filed some more. Presently the lock turned. He gave the key to the widow.

"Why, that . . . that's marvelous," she said. And she gave him a smile that set his head to humming. "How much?"

He waved his hand. "Locks," he said, "are like women. They merely want understanding." Uninvited, he seated himself on the sofa. "Don't you find such a large house lonesome at night?"

"No," she said, as though loneliness were beneath her. "Mister Peck, I've been thinking that you hardly seem the type for a crop picker."

"I do 'most everything. Mostly I'm a surgeon to sick driers, harvesters, and locks. A handyman. It's nice to know, though," he said, "that you've been thinking of me at all."

Her face, brushed by the lamp's soft fingers, colored a trifle. She might have responded, this time, but someone came noisily up the porch steps and knocked at the door. "Missus Firkus?" It was the overalled man with the hard brown face who had hired Darius. "Somebody said you were looking for me."

"It's taken care of, now. I lost the key to the safe. Mister Peck has made me a new one."

Bushong's shallow black eyes narrowed. "That's fine. Did he make himself one, too?"

Peck placed his hands on his thighs and rose to his feet. The widow interrupted hastily. "It was very good of him, and we won't thank him with insinuations. Mister Peck," she said pleasantly, "I wish you good night . . . and good picking."

Peck and the field boss stared at each other a moment. Then he took up his roll of tools and bade her good night. On the way back, he was attracted by a lantern in the trees. He threaded a narrow lane to find a chuck-a-luck game in progress on a blanket. A lickerish-appearing old man in high-water pants and a linen duster was running the game. A dozen pickers, most of them young, had their wagers on the cloth. The gambler looked up at Peck. "Get some action on your money, brother?" Peck shook his head and went on.

He was bothered a little. Two of the predictions made by the field boss down the road had already come to pass: he had paid too much for his groceries, and here was the tinhorn to trim the green and well-heeled. It all seemed out of character for a woman as lovely and intelligent as this one. Disturbed, he ate and went to bed. . . .

It must have been 2:00 a.m. when he heard the wagon on the road. It was moving slowly in the soft road dust. Dimly he discerned the dark outline of a loaded hop wagon moving up the road. Late, he reflected, to be taking hops to the drier. But that was all he thought of it until later.

In the morning, Peck got his first look at the Firkus hop yards. Just standing there, surveying the rows, made him feel as though he had his pants on backwards. The rows were not straight; they had not been suckered and stripped, so that they were ragged as a country boy's hair. The field was matted closer with dark-green hop vines than currants along a creek. The hills were about four feet apart, with eight plants to the hill. This made for an astounding denseness along the trellis, mostly of leaves, but unfortunately the driers were not buying leaves this year.

The work was easy, stripping yellow-green hops into the slatted basket until it was full, then carrying it over to the weighing stand. There was a line of four other workers when he hauled his first basket over to the stand. Elmo Bushong was weighing and giving out tickets. He had a big canvas-bound ledger balanced on a wheel of the wagon, and noted down the weight of the first two baskets.

What puzzled Darius was that he did not record the next one, and yet the fourth went down in the book.

He came up with his basket, and Bushong gave him a hard stare as he swung the hops onto the crossbar. He handed over the tickets. "Staying around long?" he asked.

"Until the hops are picked."

Bushong looked as though he might have said more, but he thrust the basket back in his hands abruptly and growled: "Move along."

Peck accepted the basket. "Don't forget to record that, will you? It might throw you off in your bookkeeping if you didn't."

Bushong gave him a stricken look.

Later, while he was moving along the trellis, painstakingly stripping the clusters into his basket, another picker paused by him. "You haven't picked here long, have you?" The picker grinned. "You don't have to pick so clean, then. They pay the same for stems and leaves as they do for hops. They rob us in the store, but we make it come out even."

Peck ate lunch in the field. He chewed on a sandwich, while his mind digested the matter of Elmo Bushong, who was overly shrewd in some things and undercooked in others. Certainly he must know clean picking from careless. Buying stems and leaves meant a double loss: at the scales, and at the drier, where a coarse load was graded down. This business of not entering some of the baskets, too. He tried to see how that would work out. Bushong paid for the hops, $1.50 out of the till meant 100 pounds of hops to weigh in at the drier. If too many hundreds of pounds did not show up, somebody was going to trace it right back to the weighing stand.

On the other hand, what if the foreman paid for these orphan baskets out of his own pocket? Then it was not on the records at all! He was out 1 1/2¢ a pound, but perhaps there was a way of disposing of the hops to his own advantage. It was at this point that Peck remembered the wagon going past in the night. It seemed credible that there was a way.

Before dinner, Peck washed in the creek; the cold bite of the water restored him. After eating, he took a stroll. His long legs carried him to where he could glimpse the lighted windows of the ranch house. He felt like an adolescent with his first crush, haunting his beloved's neighborhood for a glimpse of her. Yet he not only felt himself falling in love with Priscilla Firkus, but knew he had had a call as peremptory as a call to the ministry to set this ranch of hers in order. From trellis to weather vane, it was out of kilter. It was the happy hunting ground of rust and red spider. A man could spend a year here and not catch up.

Suddenly he saw her pass a window, and a moment later she left the house. She was walking purposefully, as she always did, and coming in the direction of the workers' tents. Peck played a hunch. He walked quickly down the edge of the field and cut across to put himself in her path. He halted in the glow of a campfire to fill his pipe. He heard her coming up.

"Why, hello!" he said.

"Oh, Mister Peck! I was looking for you. . . ." She stopped, as if that were a bald admission of dependence or something. She wore a long, dark skirt and a white, open work blouse, with ribbon woven through the cuffs and collar, and she had changed her hair-do. "You know, I hate to be forever asking help of you, but it's the kitchen pump this time. It hasn't been right in months. Now it's stopped pumping."

"Fine! I mean, that's too bad. We'll go right over."

He started to guide her toward the house, but she protested: "Won't you need your tools?"

Smiling, he patted his coat pocket. "I have an emergency kit. Around here, there is no telling when I'll need them."

She glanced at him. "Do you find my ranch so dilapidated?"

"Misused is more the word. It wants care."

121

"Mister Bushong is a good foreman," she stated, as though to remind herself as well as him. "The really important things don't break down."

"Do your account books ever break down?"

They went through the house to the kitchen. He tried the pump. It made gagging sounds, but would not pull the water up. He removed two bolts, frowning when he noticed they were not tight. He found the thick leather washer too small for the cylinder. Suddenly his heart gave a bound. The edge of it had been trimmed and then buffed to make the cut look old.

Peck fixed it, and they went back to the parlor. Priscilla said: "Do you like huckleberry pie? I . . . I happened to make one today."

"I happen not to have had huckleberry pie in two years." Peck smiled.

The pie was delicious. He ate three-quarters of it, while she smiled indulgently on him. Then he nodded at the organ. "Do you play?"

She was reluctant, but he insisted. When she played "Oh, Willie, We Have Missed You," he sang with her. It was an extremely intimate moment, until he saw Bushong's face appear at the screen door briefly, and then depart with an expression partly of hatred but mainly of hurt, of jealousy that scalded and disfigured. It was a brief and poignant look into the man's sullen heart. He was in love with the widow, too.

They sat on the sofa. Darius tried to think how to say it. Not about Bushong, but about her, for he thought he had the wistful soul of her pinned down at last like a butterfly on a board. "Missus Firkus," he said, "may I tell you something about yourself?"

She smoothed her dress, not looking up. "Do you think you can tell me anything I don't know?"

"Something you won't admit, at least. You're afraid . . . afraid of being cheated, done out of the ranch. That's why you roasted Sizemore yesterday, and I think it's why you cheat the workers on groceries."

She was back in armor immediately, stiffening against the sofa and breathing through crisply flaring nostrils. Peck shook his head and reached to hold her hand, gripping it when she tried to pull away.

"You don't do these things because you want to, but because you know that every other rancher is saying that a woman can't operate a hop yard, and you're going to show them you can, and you won't be put upon, either. It seems to me that people who make such a point of not being put upon generally are. For instance, you paid out at least twenty percent more for the picking than you should have. Your people aren't picking clean. They retaliate that way for paying too much in the commissary."

She stood up, taut-lipped. "Thank you for fixing the pump."

"You're welcome. . . . Do you trust this man, Bushong?"

She frowned. "He was with my husband, and he's the only man who's taken my part against the others since Mister Firkus died. I'm very fortunate to have him."

Peck hesitated. "I wouldn't outrightly accuse him, but . . . well, he knows those hops aren't being picked clean. He knows they'll be graded down because of it. And he's careless about stringing and poling, and has twice as many plants to the hill as anyone else."

A little crease of doubt appeared between her eyes. "Elmo says the soil is poor, and it's the only way to get a decent crop."

"Elmo is a fool, then. Or would be, if he meant it. I think he's making more money out of the ranch than you are. He fails to record every fourth or fifth basket of hops. Who gets them?"

"Who do you think gets them?" Her irony was quick and sharp.

Darius frowned. "I don't see just how he would manage that end of it, I'll admit, but I would bet that at two o'clock tomorrow morning, a wagon will leave here loaded with hops, and Bushong will be driving it."

Priscilla gasped. Her hand came smartly across his mouth. "Since Elmo isn't here to defend himself, you can take that as from him. That's a lie, and I won't have a liar on my ranch, nor a snooper, and you can leave in the morning."

Peck stood up. "I'm sorry," he said. "If I hadn't felt the way I do about you, I'd have kept still. All I stood to have out of this was a slap and I knew it. Good bye, Priscilla. You'll have better luck with that pump if you don't take the scissors to it any more."

She flushed, clenching her hands. "Oh, I've never known anyone so. . . ."

"Neither have I." Peck sighed. "That was why I took the chance."

To reach his wagon, he had to pass the barn. As he rounded it, a shape loomed up before him, and Elmo Bushong was seizing him by one arm while he swung a broken singletree at his head. Peck tore loose, throwing an arm aloft, but the club jarred his arm aside and thumped stunningly against his head. He went back against the barn and slipped down. Then he glanced up foggily, and saw Bushong looming over him with the club.

Bushong stood back a pace and half sobbed: "What are you doing to her?"

"I'm not doing anything to her. She asked me to fix the kitchen pump."

"Why was she playing the organ for you? She's never played it for me. She hasn't played it since her husband died."

"I don't know," Peck said. "I don't know why she did."

"Because she likes the sassy way you talk to her and thinks

she's in love with you!" Suddenly he was flinging coins at him. "Take those and get out! Tonight."

Peck got to his feet. "You didn't have to club me to get that across. She just fired me. I told her I thought you were robbing her."

Bushong's brown, eyebrowless face mulled it over, and lightened. "She threw you out, eh?"

"For pointing out that you either don't know how to run a hop yard profitably, or choose not to."

It was clear the widow's standing up for him encouraged Bushong immensely. He softened. "I do my best," he said earnestly. "But what can a man do when he can't make the big decisions . . . just the little ones? If I could run the place my way, it would pay."

"As her husband, you mean?"

Bushong tossed the club away. "Yes," he said, "as her husband." He walked off into the night.

Peck took down his tent, rolled his bedding, and loaded the wagon. He moved it and the horse to a new location by the woodpile. If Bushong checked on him, he would be rewarded by the patch of bare ground. He rested in the wagon for a couple of hours. Then he moved over to a clump of bird cherry beside the road, about 100 yards below the hop field. It was damp and chilly, and things moved disturbingly in the grass. But he sat there grimly on a spread-out newspaper and waited.

About 2:30 a.m., he heard a wagon moving very slowly down the road toward him. It was a moonless night, but he made out the bulk of the hop wagon between the lines of trees. A single horse was pulling it. Bushong's heavy-shouldered body was hunched on the seat. As it passed, Peck walked out, grabbed the slats of the tailgate, and climbed to the top.

Bushong drove about a mile. A man stepped out of the

shadows of another hop yard, and the foreman set the brake and jumped down. Something changed hands between them. The other man climbed up.

Bushong called up: "Nothing tomorrow night! But leave the wagon the same place."

"All right."

"What I don't understand," Darius Peck said, rising, "is how the hops can be marketed other than by a bona-fide farmer? Or are you one? I suppose that's it. You must be one of the farmers who claims a woman can't operate a hop yard profitably."

The man on the seat uttered something like a bleat and leaped to the ground. He disappeared immediately into the arbors, but the sound of his crashing along could be heard for some time.

Peck jumped down. Bushong stood there with his hands hanging. His face was without expression, blank as a slate.

"I'm sorry," Peck told him. "The things a man will do for love! You thought that if she lost enough money, she'd have to marry you to get the place farmed right. Whereas, sooner or later, she'd probably have fired you."

"Exactly," someone said—and it was the Widow Firkus, rising from the canvas in the forepart of the wagon. "I thought it was odd this wagon shouldn't have gone with the others, and I waited to see."

"Missus Firkus!" Bushong cried with real pain in his voice. "I wasn't stealing! I've got all the money. I would have given it back somehow, after. . . . It was . . . it looked like the only way, to me."

"Leave the money in your room when you go," Priscilla said.

Bushong walked slowly up the road, still, in his mind, seeming to grind on the matter of where his logic had been wrong.

"Can you drive this thing?" Priscilla called down.

Peck mounted and succeeded in turning the wagon. "You say

you can fix anything," Priscilla said. "Can you fix a run-down hop farm?"

Peck nodded his head. "Perhaps," he said. "If my heart were in it."

Sitting close to him, she said: "There's no reason why it shouldn't be."

"You wouldn't put upon me?" Peck said.

"If I did"—she sighed—"I dare say you'd know how to fix that, too."

★ ★ ★ ★ ★

HANGIN' HOBBS'S HEMP STAMPEDE

★ ★ ★ ★ ★

I

Mayor Charlie Gregg had an honest man's eyes, but his talk didn't come from an untroubled heart. His visitor sat in the juniper armchair by the window, smoking a cigar, seldom speaking, never moving more than a fat hand, but his eyes were fully alive. He was letting the mayor talk himself out. Hangin' Gus Hobbs knew that sooner or later the trouble he saw in Mayor Gregg's gray eyes would come to his lips.

They could hear the *rattle* of ore down a grizzly up at the Gopher Hole. A mule brayed, and the breeze that lifted the slatternly curtains came off warm earth and mountain cedar. The day was peaceful—and here they sat, the most notorious hangman in New Mexico Territory and the man who had sent for him, talking about trivial things and thinking about sudden death.

The hanging marshal began to weary of Mayor Gregg's conversation. He had only landed from the stage a half hour ago, and he had heard the town's history, statistics on rainfall, and three jokes about Pat and Mike since he had arrived in Mojave. He said: "You paying my fee personally, Gregg?"

The mayor shifted in his chair. "Don't worry about the money," he said. Charlie Gregg was in his fifties, his hair gray and thick, his features square. His large hands continually made meaningless adjustments of the articles on his desk.

"What about Jim Dublin?" Hangin' Hobbs said.

"Dublin?" The mayor started. "Oh, yes! About Jim. Well, of

course we have a sheriff . . . Cleve Felton . . . but Cleve hates like sin to stretch a man's neck. So I sent for you. All deference to you, Marshal." The mayor tried to smile.

Gus Hobbs waved his hand impatiently. He looked very severe, this overfed man whose eyes were as friendly as a lost pup's, who looked like a circuit rider, and whose hands were said to have hung more men than any executioner in the territory. "I'm like a doctor," Gus Hobbs said. "I like to know about my patients. I don't hang just anybody. Horse thieves and the like are a waste of my time. Why am I hanging this man?"

"The jury called it murder."

"But that ain't why you sent for me," said Hangin' Gus Hobbs. He pointed his cigar at the man behind the desk. "The next time you open your mouth," he said sharply, "I want the real reason I was sent for. Don't bother with any cock-and-bull yarns, because I've heard 'em all. You think Jim Dublin's been framed, is that it?"

Mayor Charlie Gregg went to the window and, despite the heat, closed it. He opened the door to the main portion of his establishment, a mercantile store, and made sure that no one was near the door. He said to the marshal: "Day after tomorrow an innocent man hangs, unless I can do something to save him. My daughter tells me she's through with me if Jim dances. I heard that you never hang a man till you're sure he's guilty. I thought. . . ."

"Who's Dublin supposed to have killed?" Hobbs interrupted.

"A man named Billy Ide. Billy worked for the Four As. Four As is an outfit that leases abandoned mines, sells stock for operating money, and works over the tailings for what they missed during the booms. Billy was just an old boomer doing clean-up work for the company. At first it looked like a cave-in in an old tunnel, but later on they found a bullet hole in him. And then somebody found a scrap of paper in the tunnel, bearing the letterhead of Jim's law firm. Jim had used the paper as wadding for his old Navy pistol, and it didn't burn."

Hangin' Hobbs kept his steady eyes on Gregg. He said: "Is that all?"

Gregg ran his tongue across his lips. "Billy Ide and Jim had had trouble over Billy's soundin' off. It seems that Jim thinks the Four As makes all its money by selling stock, because they haven't produced anything much but assessments. Personally I think the outfit is square enough, but Jim had a suit pending against them. Billy claimed Jim was just trying to kill the boom the Four As were starting. But they'd never had any real trouble until . . . this. I like Jim, and I can't believe he did it."

Marshal Hobbs stood suddenly. "You can't pardon a man because somebody likes him," he said. "If that's all you got to say, I can tell you this . . . Jim Dublin hangs on schedule."

Mayor Gregg swallowed. "Anyway, keep your eyes open, will you?" he said. "And . . . just as a favor . . . don't mention that I asked you to come down. It ain't popular around here to be on Jim's side."

From the porch of the Mountain View House, Hangin' Hobbs had a clear view of the town. The relics of former grandeur were still upon Mojave, recalling its youth as the queen of the silver hills, but the only silver left in town now was in its resident's teeth. Sheet-metal stamp mills and a smelter with a crumbling brick chimney occupied the north end of the town, where the street broke into a gallop up the cañon.

The mountain country of New Mexico had a hundred of these forgotten remnants of a glorious past, but Mojave had lived on because it had cattle ranches nearby and a narrow-gauge railroad that ran once a week. But even the railroad didn't make the town any more attractive to Hangin' Hobbs.

Charlie Gregg was a man you could like, but Charlie Gregg

was lying. Gus had seen enough men with soiled coattails to know what the mayor's trouble was: he had information that would possibly clear young Jim Dublin, but he couldn't disclose it without involving himself. So he'd sent for the hanging marshal from Three Rivers. Everybody in New Mexico, Gus Hobbs thought, was sending for him these days. Legends grew miraculously in the soil of the West. By official record, the hanging marshal had hung exactly two men, both confessed murderers. But any man on the street would tell you he had hung forty—or eighty, as the legend went in his particular neighborhood—and that he had saved a few innocent men in the bargain.

He sighed, looking down the porch at the heavy-shouldered man coming up the steps. A white Stetson, contrasting with a brown suit, brought attention to the man, as if the star on his chest were not enough. He took a chair beside Gus.

"You must be Gus Hobbs," he said. "I heard you were in town. Cleve Felton."

Gus shook his hand. Sheriff Felton was a ruggedly built man with too much fat under his snakeskin belt and mementos of many drinking bouts printed on his face.

The marshal remembered the mayor's plea that he be kept out of it. He said: "I hear you're hanging a man Saturday."

The sheriff, plugging tobacco into a pipe, glanced at a bench on the hillside. It was growing dusk, but the sun paused in its retreat to tie long shadows to every object on the hillside, and the shadow of the scaffold on the bench was a grim and forbidding thing.

"You can see the scaffold from here," he said. "Eight-by-eight Oregon pine with an eight-foot drop. A platform big enough to hold me and a preacher and one or two others, as well as Jim Dublin."

Hangin' Hobbs murmured: "Nice. But don't eight feet seem a little long? If the knot's snugged in right, I contend a one-foot

134

drop will do 'er."

Felton spun the match into the street. "Chancy," he said. "Besides, a three-quarter-inch rope will choke him down even if his neck ain't busted. Six of one to a half dozen of the other."

The hanging marshal winced. He held up his hands as a priest might against profanity before the pulpit. "Man!" he said. "Do you hang men for the money, or for your art?"

Felton seemed taken aback. He took the pipe from his lips. "Why, I never gave it much thought," he said. "As long as the job gets done. . . ."

Gus Hobbs stood up. "As long as a cook dishes up a steak," he said, "what's the difference whether it's medium rare or burned black? As long as an artist has got to paint a picture, why not use a kalsomine brush instead of a sable? My friend, men like you and I are privileged to perform the last earthly rite for the doomed. We can send them off jumping like a monkey on a string, or we can send them through the drop in a smooth, dignified fashion. It's a responsibility."

Felton cleared his throat. "I guess you might look at it that way. Tell you what . . . you going to be in town for the hanging?"

Hangin' Hobbs's shoulders moved. "Might."

"Well, look, then. Why not do the honors for me? I'll scare up your fee somewheres. Maybe," he added, "it'll pour a little oil on certain troubled waters if I show my good faith by sending him off in style."

The hanging marshal frowned. "I wouldn't like to dabble in anything of a controversial nature," he said. "And I haven't got the time to investigate. . . ."

Felton made a grimace. "Did anybody ever get strung up that somebody didn't holler . . . 'Wrong man'? I'll guarantee he's guilty. And it's just as well if you don't do any investigating. No use rilin' up the pool. Can I count on you, then?"

135

"I'll have to size up the prisoner," Gus said. "But tentatively . . . yes."

Hunger finally drove Gus to seek out the Antlers Grill. In Gus Hobbs's cookbook, T-bones and filets were the only food fit for human consumption, and these only when artistically prepared. For the half-inch-thick-and-well-done school he had only a thumb and forefinger clamped over the nose. He told Studhorse Shadley, the proprietor, about it before he let the man enter his kitchen.

"Cut it as thick as the family Bible," he directed, "and have your skillet red hot. Throw in a little taller, and then the steak. Warm 'er up and throw 'er on a platter."

Studhorse was a man with small round ears like half dollars shoved into the side of his bullet head. He had sloping shoulders, a simple face, and trusting eyes.

"You mean," he said, "I should cut off the tail, hoofs, and horns and run her across the frying pan. Will you rope her yourself or shall I lead 'er in?"

The hanging marshal leaned back against the upright of the booth as the man went off, smiling contentedly. Studhorse Shadley had cooked steaks before. He was back presently with two pounds of rare beef that kindness demanded should be anaesthetized before being cut.

Studhorse sat there with his chin cupped in his hands, breathing heavily through his nostrils as he watched Gus eat. His eyes were misty. The marshal ate with a gourmet's delicacy, closing his eyes with each bite.

"I only knowed one other man could punish a steak thataway," the café man said. "And he's dead now. Pore old Billy Ide."

The marshal stopped eating. "You knew him?"

Studhorse said sadly: "Reckon he ate a whole corral full of

steaks here in his time." Then he smiled. "But I'll never get paid for that last one. He didn't have the price, so he left a sack of ore samples he said was worth something. Pore old Billy. I found out later he just scrabbled 'em out around the Gopher Hole, where he was cleaning things up."

Marshal Hobbs finished the T-bone and extracted a silver toothpick from a leather case. "Who told you they weren't any good?" he said.

"Roy Bragg. He runs the Four As. Knows pay dirt from six miles away. I was showing it to Roy one night. 'Studhoss,' he says, 'give it to your wife to line her cactus garden with. That's all the good you'll ever get out of it.' It's mighty purty, though."

The restaurateur went behind the counter and came back with a sugar sack, the contents of which he dumped on the table. He turned a chunk of white porphyry over in his hand, streaked with green and black and gold. "Swear it was gold, wouldn't you?" he said.

"Sure would," Hangin' Hobbs said. "Mind if I take a chunk of it along? My wife collects colored rocks, too."

"Help yourself," said Studhorse Shadley. "The steak will be a dollar, Marshal."

II

The night was warm. Along the western hills glowed the final green rays of the sun. In a building among the ancient stopes of the dead Gopher Hole Mine a few lights were burning. Hangin' Hobbs studied the ore sample as he walked slowly back to the hotel.

This Roy Bragg must be a nice fellow, he thought. Gus knew ores a little. And he knew the ledge from which this piece had come would run $30 a ton. But if Bragg's company had the lease on the Gopher Hole, why would he have tried to cover up a rich strike? Maybe Jim Dublin would have some answers to

Frank Bonham

that, he thought.

Dublin was partially drunk when Gus talked to him. Someone had brought him a bottle of whiskey, and you couldn't blame him, in the hangman's opinion, if he had partaken too freely. Men found a host of different ways of spending their last few hours, and it was not in Hobbs's heart to censure any of them.

Sheriff Cleve Felton made a blunt introduction. "Dublin," he said, "this is Hangin' Gus Hobbs, from Three Rivers. He's going to hang you with the same rope that hung the Hueco Kid, George Parrish, and Pancho Corrales." At the door, he grinned. "No extra charge," he said.

Dublin took it emotionlessly, lying back on his cot with a cigarette in his long fingers. Hobbs looked him over. A long, spare frame, a long face with thin cheeks and dark eyes, long legs propped up on the end of the cot. He needed a shave and his eyes were bloodshot, but behind these things there was a clean, sharp look to Jim Dublin.

Hangin' Hobbs gingerly arranged his bulk on an apple box that did duty as a chair. The sheriff retreated down the corridor.

"Sheriff Felton," said the marshal, "has been kind enough to offer me the privilege of doing the honors for you." He let his eyes rove shrewdly over the lean frame on the bed, his face austere and calculating. "But now that I look you over, I ain't so sure I want the job. Too lanky. That kind makes a hangman look sloppy. You can't help him jumping around a little."

Jim Dublin threw the cigarette out the window. "Marshal," he said, "you're an old windbag. I've heard of you. You're Santa Claus in hemp. Who sent for you . . . Gregg or Nancy?"

"As a matter of fact," Gus said, "I just happened to be passing through."

Dublin sat up. "Nobody happens to pass through Mojave. It isn't on the way to anywhere. You were sent for because somebody's conscience is giving him the leapin' horrors."

Hangin' Hobbs glanced into the hall. When he turned back, the gold tooth at the corner of his mouth was shining. "You're the noticin' sort, Dublin," he said. "Mayor Gregg sent for me. And you're right about his conscience."

Dublin got up and walked across the room twice. He started to roll another smoke. "You bet I am. He's in this up to his ears. He's afraid that, if he talks, they'll kill him or impeach him."

"He links up with this Roy Bragg somewhere, don't he?" the marshal asked.

"Somewhere!" Dublin snorted. "All the way. He backed Bragg's Four As outfit when he came around selling stock. Everybody in town but me has his bottom dollar sunk in Four As stock. As city attorney, I tried to keep them from leasing the old Gopher Hole Mine, but Gregg overrode me."

"Why did you fight them?" the marshal asked him.

"Because I'd seen this shell game worked before. A promoter comes along claiming he has a new process for reclaiming gold from the tailings of old mines. He can take out millions that the original operators missed. But he'll need money to set up his equipment and hire men, so he sells stock. Lots of it. He piddles around for six months, and then he says it wasn't as rich a deposit as he figured. He packs his gilt-edge stock, and moves on to the next town. That's what Bragg is doing. He's had Henry Saxon, his attorney, start bankruptcy proceedings. You can see where that puts Mayor Gregg, in the eyes of Mojave." He paused, and then said: "Anybody but a daughter could see that he was getting his cut out of the swindle. But Nancy Gregg gave me the mitten for saying so."

Gus cleared his throat. "It wasn't exactly the act of a tactful man to mention it, son."

"I'd do it again if I had the chance," Dublin said. "Now she's thrown it right in my face by going to work for the outfit that's hanging me."

Hangin' Hobbs let a decent pause gather. "It still doesn't make it clear why Billy Ide was killed," he remarked.

Jim Dublin sat down. He said: "No. That puzzles me, too. I've been trying to work up a case against them, and it would be to their interest to knock me over. But why kill that old chlorider to do it? A bullet in my back would have been the easy way."

The marshal showed him the ore sample the café man had given him. "Does this give you any ideas? Billy Ide left a sack of this stuff with Studhorse Shadley the night before he was killed. Bragg says it's just rock."

The lawyer squinted at it, tracing the veins of color. "Rock!" he said. "That's high-grade. Where would Billy have gotten it?"

"Maybe in the Gopher Hole."

Dublin pulled his lower lip up in thought. "No. Because they started bankruptcy proceedings after his murder. If it goes through, they've lost control of the mine."

Gus Hobbs arose. "Tomorrow," he said, "I'm going to see Roy Bragg and some other people. We've got until noon, day after tomorrow, to find out who killed Billy Ide. By the way . . . I forgot to ask whether you did it."

Jim Dublin grinned. "Now, what do you think?" he said.

When he went out into the corridor, Gus Hobbs heard a light step, and looking down the gloomy hall he saw Sheriff Felton just disappearing into his office. But when he went through, the sheriff was seated at his desk going through a stack of dodgers.

In the morning Gus walked up the cañon to the Gopher Hole Mine. The office was a hot little tin shack above an old stamp mill. There were a dozen workmen about, shoveling finely crushed ore from several large wooden bins into a cyanide tank.

A couple of others were trundling wheelbarrows down the slope from one of the old tunnels. Over the whole scene hovered the despondent air of a lame-duck session.

The two men and the girl in the office, however, looked cheerful enough. The girl, who was copying a legal form on a sheet of letterpress paper, looked up at the marshal with quick brown eyes. She had light brown hair pulled back by a blue ribbon, and her lips were for smiling.

She said: "Good morning, Marshal. Did you want to see someone?"

Gus looked at the men seated at a dilapidated table, with a big gray ledger between them. One of them was stocky and had short gray hair, with a tippler's nose above a large mouth. He was smiling over some joke, his teeth showing, big and square, but there was an aggressive, unsmiling quality about the hazel eyes.

The other man was thin and had worry lines about his eyes. A yellow pencil slanted over one ear.

"Looking for Roy Bragg," the marshal said.

"I'm Bragg," the square-set man said.

Gus Hobbs introduced himself. "Understand you had some unpleasantness up here," he said. "Sheriff Felton tells me one of the boys went loco and knocked over a workman of yours."

Roy Bragg's pencil made a firm, black mark on the edge of the ledger. "That's all cleaned up now," he said. "Jim Dublin swings tomorrow."

Henry Saxon opened his mustached slice of a mouth to say: "He's been begging for it. The pig."

Hangin' Hobbs leaned on the counter, sending a glance at the girl. Nancy Gregg had her eyes on the copy she was making, but her lips pressed tightly together for an instant.

"I was thinking I might take a look at the scene of the crime," he said.

141

The lawyer, Saxon, raised his eyes. "Did Felton send you up here?"

"In a manner of speaking," said the marshal. "Hangings are a specialty of mine. I was passing through, and Felton asked me to show him how it's done in Three Rivers. So I thought I'd kill some time looking around."

Both men leaned back in their chairs to look at him, seeming relieved. "That's different," Bragg said. He got up and kicked open the swinging door in the low fence-like partition. Saxon slammed the ledger closed with a sound like a thunderclap. He followed them into the brassy sunlight.

Hobbs stopped for breath before they reached the tunnel. He wiped his sweating red face, gazing down on the cyanide tanks where ore was being slowly stirred by a couple of Mexican workmen. "Looks like there'd be money in this business," he remarked.

Roy Bragg said shortly: "There ain't. We're going into bankruptcy next week. The last outfit worked the mines over pretty thorough before they gave up."

Hobbs lighted a cigar. He puffed slowly, listening to Bragg's tale of woe, before he said: "This interests me. I've got a friend down in Three Rivers who's got a bang-up process for recoverin' gold. You can rub a double-eagle on a rock, and by golly he'll take and grind up that rock and dissolve it in some kind of corruption, and danged if he won't give you back two-bits worth of dust!"

Saxon's shrewd dark eyes wandered with some apprehension to the marshal's bland moon-face. "Well, well," he said.

Roy Bragg grunted: "If you've got your breath, let's go on and get out of this sun."

"Give me thirty seconds," Hobbs said. "I was thinking that if you want to get your money out of this, I could likely peddle the layout to this gent. He asked me to keep my eyes open for likely looking spots."

"It's too late," Saxon snapped. "Proceedings are already under way."

"They could be stopped quick enough," the marshal told him. "This way you could pay off your stockholders and take a little profit yourself."

Bragg put his thumbs in the armholes of his vest. "What makes you think there's money here, anyway?" he inquired.

"Bound to be some. Besides, the risk would all be my friend's. Can I tell him you'll talk business?"

Roy Bragg said—"No."—and continued up the trail.

III

There was relief from summer heat in the cool, dark drift that probed deep into the hill. At the first side drift Roy Bragg handed the lantern to the marshal. "It's straight back about three hundred yards," he said. "There's nothing to see, but go on back if you want. We're knocking off for lunch. Be at the Antlers if you need us."

Gus Hobbs watched them move down the shaft, neat black silhouettes against the glaring rectangle of the portal. He put the lantern down and stood there studying. By his refusal to sell the Gopher Hole lease, Roy Bragg had built his own scaffold, as far as Hangin' Gus Hobbs was concerned. A man didn't go into bankruptcy because he wanted to. He did so because he was forced into it by his creditors. But Bragg had chosen to let the Four As go broke rather than sell out to Hangin' Gus's mythical buyer.

It added up to this: Billy Ide had run across a ledge of rich ore in cleaning up one of the Gopher Hole drifts. Roy Bragg, bless the carpetbagger's soul of him, had chosen to keep the find for himself by eliminating the old miner and letting the lease go. Later he would come back, or have an agent come back, and file on the claim, cutting a lot of unhappy stockholders out of their share.

Hobbs knew something else now. Billy Ide hadn't been working in this tunnel when he was killed, because the decades-old rubble on the floor was undisturbed by the marks of wheelbarrow or mule car. Probably he had been killed elsewhere and brought here to be found. Gus started down the tunnel to check on his theory.

Every 100 feet or so he passed a side drift, or a raise, and, when he finally came to the end of the tunnel, it was directly under a shaft that ascended into echoing blackness. At some time ore had been cascaded down this raise to be loaded into cars and hauled to the grizzly. By the light of the lantern Gus found some old brown bloodstains on a rock.

There was something about the black hole over his head that disturbed him. Maybe it was a sound. Maybe just the cool, dry breeze that soughed through it like a woman's sigh. At any rate he experienced a sudden compulsion to get out from under it.

A moment later the slide occurred.

It began with a muffled *boom* far above, and then, rattling and roaring, an avalanche of rocks and dirt thundered down the shaft and mushroomed on the floor of the tunnel. Gus felt the lantern torn from his grasp by a flying rock, and in the terror-shot blackness he began to run. The dust was in his windpipe, in his eyes. He was not a man who liked exercise, but he broke some sprinting records before he careened against the wall and went down.

He sat up. The dust was like clay in his mouth. He thought with a shiver of panic that the grave must be like this—blackness and solitude, and the taste of earth on the tongue. And if Roy Bragg had dynamited the other end of the drift, this was indeed his grave.

For a time, letting the tempo of his heart quiet, he did not try to walk. He was not even sure which way to start. In the darkness, every point of the compass was north. The rocks were still coming down in a rattling trickle. It was this fact that pointed the direction of escape.

He stumbled along, his hand on the wall, following the turns of the tunnel. No ray of light, no warm earthly sound came to tell him that he was not walled in with the rats and a gentleman called Death. It was cold, but there was sweat on the marshal's body.

He stopped. From far away, a sound came to him. Gus Hobbs eased his .44 out of the holster. The sound came again, closer, and he knew it was Nancy Gregg's voice. "Marshal . . . Marshal Hobbs?"

Gus walked ahead until he passed a turn, and then he could see her coming down the drift carrying a lantern. She was alone.

"Right here, ma'am," he said.

When she reached him, he saw that her eyes were big with fright. "I came as soon as I dared," she said. "I was sure they'd killed you. I came up as soon as they left for town."

"I asked for it," the marshal said in disgust. "They held out a noose for me and I stuck my neck in it. Let's walk. I got a feeling that these walls are just achin' to hug me."

They started back, one on each side of the strap-iron rails. Nancy Gregg talked breathlessly.

"I saw them go to the powder magazine and then walk up to an old stope above the one you were in. I wanted to warn you, but there wasn't a thing I could do."

Gus looked at her, liking the frank way she talked. "I'm trying to figure you out," he said. "Jim Dublin tells me you're sweet on Roy Bragg. But I saw the way you looked when Saxon called Jim a pig. Whose axe are you grinding?"

"Jim's," Nancy told him. "Though he'd never believe it. While he was fighting against the Four As, I didn't want anything to do with him. He was saying that Dad was mixed up in it with them, and I couldn't believe it. After Billy Ide was killed, I began to wonder. Then I took this job with Roy Bragg to see what I could find out."

They were at the portal of the tunnel now, standing in the hot, dry air that stimulated Gus Hobbs's blood like alcohol. Not until he was 100 feet from the mine did apprehension take its hand off his shoulder.

The door to the office was locked, but Nancy Gregg had a key. She opened it. "I'll show you what I found out," she said.

She went through a file of correspondence and pulled out a letter under the name of an assayer's firm. Hangin' Hobbs read it. It confirmed what he had already been certain of. Billy Ide had struck pay dirt. He said to the girl: "This will help. We can stick Roy Bragg behind the bars if he goes through with his bankruptcy scheme now. But it won't make Jim Dublin any less dead. There's just one man who can help us there."

Nancy Gregg made herself busy replacing the correspondence. "I know," she said. "My father. And I'm not even sure he knows."

Hangin' Hobbs appeared at the jail after lunch. "Guess we'll test that hangin' rig of yours," he said to Cleve Felton. He had a small leather grip with him in which he carried his hang rope.

Felton brought a sack of sand from behind the jail. They had a Mexican carry it up the hill to the scaffold. The sheriff watched with interest while Marshal Hobbs carefully shook out his rope and made the free end fast to the gibbet. He cinched the noose, with its ominous thirteen bights, about the sandbag, placing the bag at the edge of the hole through which the condemned man would plunge.

"There ought to be a trap," he said, frowning.

"The carpenter wanted five bucks to put one in," Felton said apologetically. "Usually I just give the man a kick."

The hanging marshal groaned. "Where's the dignity of your office?" he demanded. "That's like a preacher would throw a coffin in a grave upside down. I'm beginning to wish I hadn't took on this job."

Very gently he pushed the sandbag through the hole with his foot. The bag plummeted down, came to a jolting stop with a *crack* of straining hemp. Hangin' Hobbs looked down. The sack was swinging and dancing with grim realism. He sat on the railing and lit a cigar.

"Terrible," he said. He gestured to the Mexican, who hauled the sack up.

Before the rope could be tested again, men were streaming up the slope from the town, drawn by the crack of the rope. In the first group to arrive was gray-haired Mayor Charlie Gregg. Gregg's face was pasty and his eyes were like dead things.

"Marshal!" he said. "Why didn't you tell me you were stepping the hanging up a day? My God, if I'd known . . . !"

Hangin' Hobbs kicked the sandbag through the square again. Gregg and the others jumped back, startled. Gregg looked like he might collapse.

"Just testin'!" the marshal called down. "What was it you were about to say, Gregg?"

Roy Bragg and Henry Saxon appeared from the vicinity of the Antlers. Saxon still had a napkin tucked in his collar. Mayor Gregg looked at them, a trifle paler.

"Nothing," he said. "I . . . I was startled, was all." He went down the hill, a lonely, shambling figure.

Gus Hobbs smiled at Roy Bragg. "Hello, Bragg," he said.

Bragg had a shield of nonchalance that was like cast-iron. He put a smile on his lips and stood there *jingling* some keys in his pocket, just as though he hadn't tried to kill Gus a few hours ago. "Find anything up at the mine?" he said.

147

Hobbs said: "Not quite." He let them interpret the remark however they wanted. The crowd, cheated out of a show, went away grumbling. Gus gave the Mexican a $10 gold piece.

"Find yourself a *compadre,* Pancho," he said, "and keep on dropping that thing until midnight. I think the noise might help some people sleep tonight."

There was celebrating at the Buckhorn Bar that night. Men who thought Jim Dublin a murderer drank to his death; those few friends the young lawyer still had drank to forget. Marshal Hobbs and the sheriff had a table to themselves. At the bar the drinks were on Roy Bragg. The only sour note in the party was a certain sound of straining timbers and stretching rope that came at fifteen-minute intervals. Each time it came a few drinks were spilled, and a few men lost some of the lusty color the whiskey had loaned them.

At 11:00 p.m. Sheriff Cleve Felton said testily: "How long do we have to stand that racket, hangman? Some of the boys are gettin' edgy."

"It's a new rope," Gus said. "I've got to be sure it isn't going to stretch till Dublin's feet are on the ground." He finished his beer and pushed back the chair. "Let's go down to the Antlers," he said. "I feel the need of some rare beef."

Felton said—"My God!"—but when the marshal departed, he was right behind him. They had only gone as far as the entrance when the slatted doors slammed open. There in the doorway stood Mayor Charlie Gregg. Gregg was in his shirt sleeves, his gray hair disarranged, his eyes wild as he confronted the man from Three Rivers.

"All right, Marshal," he said. "You can stop them, now. You knew you'd break me. I killed Billy Ide and planted the evidence to incriminate Jim Dublin."

The only sound in the Buckhorn was the gurgle of a forgotten beer keg. Roy Bragg came from the bar. He held Gregg by the shoulder.

"You're drunk, Charlie," he said. "I guess that noise has got us all a little upset. Go on back to your office and forget about it."

It was fear, and not drunkenness, that caused the mayor to strike off his hand and back away. "No! I'm telling you the truth, Marshal. I killed him!"

Bragg smiled, as though to humor him. "Sure," he said. "But why?"

Gregg said: "Never mind that. Lock me up, Felton, and let that poor kid out of there."

Hangin' Hobbs had a feeling that what Mayor Gregg feared was not the gallows, but Roy Bragg. He thought Gregg might have a much different story to tell, once he was safely behind the bars.

He pulled his gun and placed it against the mayor's ribs. "Let's go, Sheriff," he said. "I figured somebody would break down, if I kept that rope singing long enough. We'll have a hanging tomorrow, but Jim Dublin's going to be a spectator."

The sheriff, looking dubious, took Charlie Gregg by the arm and led him from the saloon. Roy Bragg and his lawyer managed to be on either side of the pair as they went down the boardwalk, the marshal following. There was some low, intense conversation going on, which Gus could not hear. But when they reached the jail, Sheriff Felton hurried the mayor into a cell and came back with a purposeful jaw.

"That closes the case," he said. "And I'm dang' glad of it. I never did want to see Jim hang. It'll be a pleasure to hang this double-damned Judas. I guess you can go on back to Three Rivers any time you want, Marshal."

Gus waved a deprecating hand. "No hurry at all," he said. "I'd just as soon hang around till after the party. I'll take the noon stage." He started toward the door to the cell-block. "Thought I might have a talk with Gregg, though."

Felton moved to block the door. "Not necessary," he said. "Saxon, here, will take his confession."

Gus Hobbs knew a dead-end cañon when he saw one, and from experience he knew that the only way to get by such a barricade was to back up and try another trail. "Just as you say," he agreed. "But I'll wait and walk back with Dublin."

The sheriff could have no objection to this. Jim Dublin was led out, too befuddled to have any comment. From his desk the sheriff produced the lawyer's belongings—a gun, some money, and a hat. Marshal Hobbs took him up to the Antlers. When trouble crowded him closely, beefsteak was his bulwark against the world. It was the one thing that never let a man down. Women were fickle, whiskey was a forked tongue, but a T-bone was a staff to lean on.

"Jimmy," Marshal Hobbs said, "this thing is getting out of hand."

Jim Dublin sliced off a cube of pink meat. "From where I'm sitting things seem to be pretty well under control," he said. The shadows were gone from his eyes and the hard set of his mouth had relaxed.

"Charlie Gregg didn't kill Ide," Gus told him. "He only said that to get himself locked up, where he could give me the straight of it without being assassinated. But it didn't work. Felton won't let him talk to me. If I just knew what he was trying to say. . . ."

"That old windbag," Jim Dublin grunted. "Any time he admits a crime he didn't commit to save somebody else's hide, I'll ride my horse side-saddle."

"Then you can start any time you want," someone said.

They looked up to see Nancy Gregg beside the booth. She was wearing a heavy jacket against the crisp night air. Her lips were a tight line and her eyes were incandescent.

Dublin was unimpressed by her fury. "If he's playing the game straight," he said, "why didn't he come through sooner?"

"Maybe he was waiting for something to turn up," Nancy said. "Maybe he thought the murderer would confess."

"As it happens," Dublin said, "the murderer did. Unfortunately he was it."

Nancy sat beside Hangin' Hobbs. She kept her hands tightly clenched in her lap. "And to think what I've been going through for you," she said bitterly.

"I heard about that, too," Jim Dublin snorted. "Drawing wages from the man that framed me."

Gus Hobbs scowled and shoved away his steak, only half finished. "I'm no matchmaker," he said, "but it seems to me we might get further if you two came to some understanding."

Nancy bounced up again. She said: "Understanding? I'll never have one with Jim Dublin until he gets my father out of jail. I came here to tell you that Bragg is leaving town right after the hanging. He wants me to elope with him. He's going to push the bankruptcy case through at the county seat and file claim notices on the mine the same day. He's taking away all the books so there can't be any case made against him. Now," she said, "I'm through. You can make what you want out of it."

They heard her sobbing when she reached the door. Dublin started to rise, but Gus pushed him back.

"You'll have plenty of time for that tomorrow," he said. "We've got some things to do tonight. Unless Charlie Gregg gets a chance to open his mouth at the hanging, it's up to us to find out what he was trying to tell me."

"We're not mind-readers," said Dublin. "Where do we start?"

"At the scaffold. I've got some alterations to make. After that I'm open to suggestion."

IV

By 6:00 a.m., with the sunrise streaming golden over the mountains upon the cañon town, they had done nothing more constructive than to catch two hours' sleep. For breakfast, Hangin' Hobbs had a cigar. Even this did not taste right. It was in every tick of the clock that an innocent man would die today unless he produced a murderer.

Some of the curious were already sitting around the scaffold, watching Fry, the photographer, take pre-hanging shots. At 8:00 a.m., the semi-weekly stage rolled in for a five-hour lay-over before beating back down the valley. Gus sat on the gallery of the Mountain View House, watching the citizens of Mojave begin to take up the ordinary trend of their daily living. But at noon, if he knew human nature, every shop would be locked and the good townspeople would throng to the hanging like buzzards about a slaughterhouse.

Time kept on sloughing away, and there was nothing Gus could do to slow it down one second. About 11:00 a.m., a squarish figure caught his eye among the pedestrians on the board sidewalk across the street. Roy Bragg, white Stetson on his head, a cowhide suitcase in hand, sauntered into the stage office. The marshal had an idea. He stood up.

"We've been invited up to the Four As office," he told Jim Dublin. "Maybe Bragg hasn't got away with those books yet. We've still got an hour."

They walked north, following the bend of the cañon, and then taking the trail up to the Gopher Hole Mine. Among the stopes and sheet-metal structures there were no workmen today. Nevertheless they approached the office carefully. But when Gus looked through the dusty window, he saw no one but Henry Saxon, industriously burning papers in a wastebasket. They went inside and watched him for a moment. Saxon was cool, his dark, lanky features confident.

For a moment the only sound was the *crackling* of the flames. Gus began to work at his teeth with the silver toothpick. "We came to lock a barn door," he said, "but I think that's our horse you're burning there."

Saxon smiled. "I wouldn't be surprised if it were," he said.

"This makes it unpleasant," the hanging marshal said. "I don't think my nerves would stand two hangings in one day."

Saxon straightened, losing his smile. "Is somebody else being hung?" he asked.

Hangin' Hobbs sighed. "I'm afraid so. You."

Jim Dublin saw the play. He put his gun gently against the lawyer's body while Hobbs opened the door, and the three of them went quietly from the office.

Gus selected a drift high up on the hill, where they were sure of finding a winze several hundred feet deep. A five-minute walk into one of the tunnels brought them to a covered winze, a vertical shaft that led down to some tunnel far below. He threw an end of the rope over a roof timber and made it fast, tying the other end about Saxon's neck so that there was a bare six inches of slack. Then he made his hands fast behind him. All of the boards covering the winze were dragged away except a single four-by-four.

Saxon began to talk, summoning invective, legal phraseology, and appeals to common humanity. He was too good a lawyer to die quietly.

"You can save your breath for when you'll need it," Gus told him. "I'm not interested in what the Constitution or Blackstone has to say. All I know is that you know who killed Billy Ide, and how and where. I want a written confession before we leave. We've got about fifteen minutes for you to make up your mind."

Saxon began—"A confession secured under duress. . . ."—but caught his breath as he found himself prodded out over six square feet of blackness a few hundred feet deep.

153

"You can talk any time you want to," Hangin' Hobbs said. "Jim has a pencil and paper."

Saxon suddenly developed a surprising and courageous stubbornness. He clamped his mouth shut and would say nothing. Jim Dublin tried questioning and cursing, but neither had any effect.

Saxon spoke once: "If I die, I die a martyr."

"But your tongue will hang out just as far," Gus told him.

"As far as I know," the lawyer said, "Charlie Gregg is the murderer." But there was sweat on his face and his voice was going up in pitch.

Gus Hobbs stared at him, then turned away disgustedly. "We're milking a dry cow, Jimmy," he said. "We might as well go back." He picked up the lantern, and they started off down the tunnel.

Saxon spoke with some shrillness. "What about me?"

Gus's voice came back from the little cosmos of light and warmth they were carrying away with them by the bail of a lantern. "Oh, they'll find you eventually."

They passed a turn. Darkness came creeping back to the tunnel from the crannies where it had hidden. Darkness and panic-infested loneliness. They had not gone far when Henry Saxon screamed.

"Hobbs! Come back! I'll . . . !"

The cry ended. Gus Hobbs ran back, to find Saxon leaping and jackknifing at the end of the short rope, fighting to get his feet back on the timber. He pulled the lawyer over to solid ground and cut the rope. Saxon crouched on the floor, gasping, fingering his bruised neck. Gus jerked him upright.

"What's the story?" he said.

Saxon croaked: "Bragg did it! Billy Ide brought us up to Number Seven tunnel to show us the ledge he'd found, and Roy figured there'd be more money for us if he could cut the

154

rest out. He got an old letter of Jim Dublin's from Gregg and tore off part of the letterhead for wadding. He used an old Harper's Ferry rifle. That way he thought he'd get rid of both of them."

Hobbs said to Jim: "You got that down?" He took the paper from the lawyer and, placing it on a plank, watched while Saxon signed the confession. He stuffed it in his pocket and reached for the lantern. "Now, we'll be getting down there for the show," he said.

"I'll run ahead," Jim said. "Maybe I can make a little better time than you."

"No rush," Gus told him. "We'll make it all right."

When they reached daylight, they could see that Charlie Gregg was being brought up the hill to the scaffold. It was a half mile back to town, and the heat did not make traveling any faster. Gus hurried along on his short legs, the sweat rolling out of him, but before they gained the town he knew that they would be too late. Jim saw it, too, and he suddenly left them and began to sprint on those long, gangling legs of his.

Gus stopped running. It was too hot, and it was his nature to let his brain work for his body, anyway. Things were probably better under control down there than young Jim Dublin realized, even though the preacher had stepped back and the rope was being fitted about Charlie Gregg's neck. Gregg seemed to be struggling a little. His head was hooded and a man stood at each side of him to keep him from breaking loose.

Dublin reached the road above the scaffold just as Sheriff Felton placed his man beside the trap. The lanky figure halted; his gun came out and a single shot popped in the stillness as Jim fired in the air to get attention. Sheriff Felton glanced up— and very quickly he shoved the doomed man through the trap door.

Dublin put his hand over his eyes. Even Henry Saxon, walk-

Frank Bonham

ing ahead of the marshal, gasped. But Hangin' Hobbs, not slow-
ing his pace, only muttered: "The man ain't hurt. Only shook
up some."

They were close enough now to see the mob of spectators
surge back to the man struggling in the dust. Something had
gone wrong—the famed hang rope, killer of the Hueco Kid and
so many other desperados, had broken!

Someone set Gregg on his feet, despite Sheriff Felton's shouts
to give him clearance. Gus Hobbs saw Roy Bragg up on the
platform, and he knew suddenly that the time was about run
out. He was going to have to sprint after all.

Henry Saxon was a problem, but he disposed of him by tap-
ping him behind the ear with the barrel of his Colt. Then he ran
on, arriving at the scaffold in time to see the hood yanked from
Charlie Gregg's purple face. He hoped Gregg would appreciate
what he had done, in cutting through all but a few strands of
his favorite hang rope last night, just to save the man's not-too-
deserving carcass.

Gregg began to shout, pointing up at Roy Bragg, on the
platform.

"Grab him! I tried to tell you last night that he killed Billy
Ide! I got proof in my safe. Bragg tore the letterhead off a letter
of Jim Dublin's while he was in my office one day. Out of curios-
ity I saved the other half. If it don't match up with the wadding
Bragg claims he found in the tunnel, I'll let you hang me all
over again!"

Suddenly Roy Bragg had his gun in his hand, and Gregg was
running for shelter.

Hobbs said, across the barrel of his gun: "It's a rope or a bullet, Bragg. Your choice."

Bragg swerved to confront the marshal. He had Sheriff Felton for moral support, for Felton knew he was in it as deeply as
any of them. Bragg fired, the bullet snarling off the ground

156

behind Marshal Hobbs. Gus was a sparing man with lead; he always squeezed off his shots with care, preferring results to noise. When the .44 thrust against his palm, Roy Bragg went back a step and dropped through the trap.

Sheriff Felton, a look of injured amazement on his face, let his arm drop at his side, the Colt dangling from his finger by the trigger guard. He clutched at the railing for support, and then, still gripping it, slumped to the floor. Gus looked up the hill and saw Jim Dublin standing there with a smoking gun in his hand.

Mayor Charlie Gregg, his daughter, and young Jim Dublin were at the stage station when Hangin' Hobbs came from the hotel in response to the blare of the stage horn. It was just like always, Gus thought gloomily, everybody was happy but Hangin' Hobbs. Somebody was wearing a necktie instead of a rope; somebody else had his arm around a pretty girl. Everything was fine, except that he had a 200-mile jouncing stage ride ahead of him and he didn't even have his hangman's fee yet.

Mayor Gregg came forward with a parcel under his arm. He had a look on his face as though he were about to dedicate a new jail.

"I believe we owe you something more than our thanks," he said to Gus. He dropped ten $5 gold pieces into the marshal's hand. "This was a double hanging, you recall."

Gus said—"Thanks, Gregg."—and pocketed the money. He put his foot on the step, but Charlie Gregg had not finished.

The parcel, a flat bundle wrapped in an old Albuquerque newspaper, came forward. "In token of our esteem," he said.

The horses were getting restless, and Gus Hobbs grunted another word of thanks and climbed into the coach a moment before the wheels began to turn. Mojave quickly became a blur in the dust.

After a while Gus was drawn from his morose reflections by the discovery that the newspaper-wrapped bundle was growing warm and greasy. He sniffed, a well-remembered odor going through and through him. Almost trembling, he unwrapped the package. It was a T-bone to end T-bones—two inches thick, bubbling fragrant juices, grilled to a soul-wringing brown.

Tears came to Gus's eyes. He had a few soft spots in his hangman's soul, and this hit him right where he lived. Tucking the newspaper into his collar like a bib, he began to eat.

Outside, the hills that had been brown were green. The air, that had smelled of road dust, brought him the fragrance of piñon and sage. He would, he reckoned, have to come back here sometime. Nice country and nice people. And danged nice steaks!

★ ★ ★ ★ ★

THE LONG FALL

★ ★ ★ ★ ★

Voss came in. When he opened the door, you could hear the violent noises of the sawmill. Voss took both himself and lumbering very seriously. "Toughie ain't come down yet, Mister Martin," he said.

Russ Martin, deep in the theory of how to keep creditors happy though waiting, said: "Well, let me know when he does. He's got to learn that he's driving a logging truck, not an excursion bus."

Voss looked out the window. There were barrack-like piles of lumber, a stretch of open ground, and then a timbered slope ascending precipitously to the high ridges. But all the foreman saw was the dirty-green pond with its sodden flotsam of logs.

"Pond's going to be empty in another week, Mister Martin," he said.

"No, it isn't. I'm going up and raise hell with Stevens today. I told him last week he'd have to get those logs moving."

When he was upset, Voss made sounds with his plates like a horse chewing a bit. "I know what I'd do," he said. "Can him."

"And how soon do you think I could find another contractor this late in the season?"

"I'll bet," Voss said, "Stevens's daughter could tell you something about this. Her and Toughie was out last night. I hear there was a fight between him and some logger."

"Well, that's their business," Russ said. Still, the mention of Janey Stevens was like a step missed in the dark. Russ capped his fountain pen. "I'll drive up," he added.

Down in the Sacramento Valley some harried fruit growers were writing tearful letters to him. You couldn't ship fruit without boxes, and the boxwood was still up in the mountains with birds nesting in it. Russ had commitments that were liable to cost him something unless that wood came down.

Last year, by a magnificent system of mortgages and a minimum outlay of cash, he had acquired a Sierra Nevada forest lease and a sawmill. He had given Stevens the contract for cutting and hauling the logs. The dovetailing of assets and liabilities was a piece of cabinetry that a single pull might destroy. Unless Stevens's trucks began to bring those logs in, his cabinetry would be spoiled when the first note fell due.

The seat of the dusty command car was blistering. Russ roared up the log road mounting steeply from the green-black gorge of the Yuba River. He wished he could worry about it all as conscientiously as Voss. But when he worried, it wasn't over lumber. It was over Janey Stevens.

Janey was not precisely what he had in mind for a future wife. When he was out with her, he felt like an old gaffer trying to keep up with a chorus girl. And he was no old gaffer. Of course, sometimes she would be sober for a moment, not laughing, not making conversation, just being quietly natural. Those were the dangerous moments, the ones Russ knew could make him serious toward her.

Russ swung around a timbered point and found the truck. The big orange cab was still on the road, but the rear wheels of the trailer had slid into a turn. Someone stepped from the cab when he stopped. It wasn't Toughie; it was Janey.

"Where's Toughie?" Russ demanded.

"He didn't get back from town last night," Janey told him. "Pop couldn't spare another man, so I tackled it myself. Came into that one a little too fast, didn't I?" She was being very sober now. Janey was twenty-two, with dark hair and eyes and high-key coloring. She had the figure to wear sweaters and skirts, and knew it.

Russ looked at the jumble of logs sprawling from the trailer. He said: "You mean he knew you were going to take it?"

Janey said: "My goodness, I'm of age! If they hadn't put that last log on, I think I could have handled it. It's a shame about Toughie. He got tough with the wrong one. Somebody tried to cut in on us and he hit him. They took him to the hotel after it was over."

Russ had to turn his attention forcibly to the problem of getting the trailer back on the road. After a half hour of strong-arming the Diesel back and forth, he was able to free it. Then he found that the twisting had snapped the trailer extension. He said: "So now it goes into the garage."

He opened the door for her; she smiled a demure—"Thank you."—but her manner was as contrite as a tweak on the ear. "I'm sorry," she said. "I thought I could help by driving down."

"That seems to be your trouble, doesn't it?" Russ said. "If you'd slow down before you jumped into things, you might. . . ." He stopped.

"I might . . . what?" She watched him with a stiff little smile.

Russ had to backtrack. After all, it was none of his business. "I didn't mean to get philosophical." He smiled. "In fact, if your father hauls fifty thousand feet tomorrow, I'll forgive both of you."

"I tremble," she said, "with anticipation."

Why should it matter that she was angry? Yet it did matter. Lightly his hand dropped over hers. "Let's forget it," he said. "And how about trembling over a steak and a movie tonight? The truck will have to go down anyway."

Janey pursed her lips. "Well, I might," she said.

163

★ ★ ★ ★ ★

Al Stevens was operating the jammer, jockeying the last log aboard the trailer of the second truck. He cut the engine and jumped down. It was lunchtime. He and Russ went over to the cabin. Stevens was in his middle years, a hearty man with ruddy features and gray hair cut close. The story about the truck took his smile quickly enough.

"I told her she couldn't handle it! The thing is costing me fifty bucks a day whether it runs or not."

They went into the cabin, a crumbling relic of the day when some miner had camped here. Curtains and new paint gave it a pertness out of character with the decayed flooring. Russ lit a cigarette.

He said bluntly: "We might as well lay the cards on the table, Al. Am I going to have any logs to saw next week or not?"

Stevens frowned as he filled his pipe. "You are," he said, "if I can get any action out of my fallers. I'm not a man to pass the buck, but, damn it, I can't haul a log until it's cut. The falling's running a month behind."

It was the first Russ had heard of falling trouble. The fallers were Stevens's responsibility, since he had subcontracted the work. "Why don't you jack them up?" he demanded.

"The Kemble boys don't jack easy. Those two clowns ought to be able to keep a month ahead of me. I'll tell them tomorrow they've got to produce or quit."

Janey came to the kitchen door. An odd look passed between her and her father. On her part, it was a hard little thrust with disapproval in it. Then she turned and Russ saw her pick up a water bucket and go out the back door.

Stevens cleared his throat. "I was wondering if you'd like to find somebody to take over this contract of mine." When Russ merely stared, he explained. "You run into a set-up like this sometimes. I don't know what it is. Nothing seems right, nobody

164

makes any money. When that happens, the best thing seems to be to break it up."

Russ gave him a long, studying glance. "Seems to me you're making it pretty complicated. If the Kembles are all that are holding you back, why haven't you done something about them before now?"

Stevens hesitated. Then he grinned. "I told Janey there was no pulling the wool over your eyes. You may as well have it, Russ. I'm a low-down gyppo . . . a thirty-day logger. I haven't spent over three months on a job in twenty years. I thought maybe, if I got into something of my own, I'd stick around long enough to line my wallet. But now the wind's talking to me again, and I've got the itch to hear what it's saying."

Russ said: "I'm sorry, Al. But if you leave me holding the bag, I'll see that you don't work any camp in California for a long time."

"Suppose I find somebody to take over my contract?"

"If you want to stand behind them."

Stevens rubbed his jaw. "I know some boys in Oregon that might take it over. I'll write them."

Russ was disturbed. He found it hard to picture this bluff, easy-going Irishman as a transient worker. The idea of Janey's leaving was unsettling, too.

Janey came back and they sat down to eat. Russ noticed a photograph on a shelf, one of those embalmed sepia portraits. It was of a good-looking boy about twenty. "Relative?" he asked.

Stevens looked at the picture. "That was my boy, Ed. He was killed two years ago."

Russ was sorry he had spoken.

"I guess," Stevens said, "it comes to all of us that haven't got enough sense to get out of the trade. He was a rigger."

It was all that needed to be said. There was a saying that riggers didn't die because they fell so far, but because they landed so fast.

Russ had a room in the hotel at Washington, a ghost town across the river from the mill. At 4:00 p.m. he changed his clothes and returned to the mill. Already the cañon had entered its brief summer twilight. Janey Stevens rode down with the driver of the other truck.

They walked out to the pond, where his car and the truck were parked. The way her dark hair moved gently on her shoulders, the young clean grace of her body made him forget everything but the luxury of being with her.

Voss and another man were on the pond, poling out to a half-submerged log. Things were bad when they had to retrieve sinkers.

"What'll you drive?" Russ asked her. "A Chevy coupe or a Diesel that handles like an Irish Mail?"

"I'll take the Chevy. I haven't driven an Irish Mail in weeks." She slid under the wheel and started the motor. Russ lingered. Then he realized she was watching Voss and the other man on the pond.

Suddenly he heard Voss shout. He turned in time to see him stagger from the log and disappear under the brown surface scum. He saw the tongs, tracing a wild arc at the end of the high line, swing away from him. He knew what had happened. Somebody had brought them up behind the foreman without warning.

The other man on the log lost his balance and plunged in, too. He came up instantly, but Voss stayed under.

The car with Janey at the wheel moved away so suddenly that Russ, still leaning on the door, was whirled around. It shot away, the tires hurling gravel, made a skidding turn, and crossed the lot. It was still gathering speed when it hit the road. Russ swore, watched a moment, and ran to the edge of the pond.

The man out there kept yelling for help. He was clinging to the slowly revolving log with one hand and dragging something up out of the water with the other. Voss's head came into view. The workman had him by the hair. Russ started out over the logs, moving with a sure, practiced grace. Others were coming out, too. Among them, they were able to get the foreman across a log and move it in.

Voss came around in a few minutes. Color surged back to his face. "Damn greenhorn mill hands!" he swore. "I wouldn't give you four bits for all of 'em in California. Well, what're you standing around for?" he demanded. "We're makin' lumber, ain't we?"

Russ, walking back to the truck, was still cold with the shock of what he had seen in Janey's eyes.

Now, at last, he knew that it wasn't Al Stevens who was the thirty-day logger, but Janey. Janey, to whom the violence and danger of the woods was like a dark pocket in her mind.

He drove the truck as fast as he dared. He reached the highway, and after that it was straighter running.

Maybe he was overexcited. Maybe it was normal for a girl to run like that from an accident. He didn't think so. He thought she was running away from something that had happened long ago. He remembered what Al Stevens had said: That was my boy, Ed. *He was killed two years ago. I guess it comes to all of us. . . .*

He reached Nevada City in an hour and drove to the garage. His car was in front of the garage with Janey still at the wheel. He left the truck and hurried outside. Janey got out and consulted her watch.

"I've been waiting," she said, "exactly thirty-nine minutes."

"And I've been waiting," Russ said, "to find you piled up in the ditch."

Janey laughed. You could forget how terrified she had been, if you were willing to accept the sham she displayed. She took his arm and they started up the steep main street.

"Aren't you curious about whether we pulled Voss out?" he asked.

"You wouldn't be here if you hadn't. How is he?"

"Alive and mad. Why did you run off like that?"

"I've seen them hurt before. I hate it. It's the way I am."

They went into the Clover Leaf. The food wasn't much, but Janey liked it because it had the only juke box outside of the saloons. She objected when he started to guide her to a booth. "Aren't you going to buy me a drink after hauling logs for you all day?"

At the bar, he glanced at her, perched on the high chrome stool with her heels caught on the rung. He knew by now that direct questions would get him nothing. Yet he was not willing to drop it. He said: "This is the third time we've been out, but all I know about you is that you love hot jazz and you can't drive a truck for sour apples."

"A word picture," she said. "But let us not forget that I graduated *magna cum laude* from Cedarville High. I'm the one in front who shut her eyes just as the camera clicked. And I like Mozart as well as I like Mugsy Spanier, so there! I like olives, too, only I get so tired of drinking those old Martinis to get them. In fact, I like about everything except people who call me baby."

"And the trees," Russ added.

Her glance was quizzical.

"You forgot the trees. You don't like them, either, do you?"

Someone had fed a nickel into the juke box. Janey slipped down off the stool. "I'm sorry I'm not psychic. I guess I'd have to be, to get that one." She held out her hands.

Russ was outmaneuvered. They danced. In his arms she was

light and warm and exciting.

Just before the music ended, Russ said: "Janey, let's stop sparring. My heart didn't beat from the time you ran away until I found you."

" 'Your heart stood still. . . .' That's from 'Connecticut Yankee', isn't it?"

"I don't know what it's from. But this is from me. You're acting. You've been acting for two years, ever since you saw your brother killed. That's why you ran today, isn't it?"

She was out of his arms with a little wrench. "I don't know whether it was or not. And I'm not sure it's any of your business." She walked to the bar and retrieved her bag.

Russ caught up with her. He said: "Janey, please. . . ." And then she put her hand on his arm.

"Why, there's Harry Kemble!"

Kemble, elder of the two brothers to whom Stevens had let the falling contract, was standing near the door. He approached them, a blond humorless man with gray eyes in a long, tanned face. He glanced at Russ, then turned to Janey.

"Am I going to have to buy you a date book?" he asked.

"Harry! It wasn't tonight . . . ?"

"This is Friday, isn't it?"

Janey glanced at Russ, coloring. Russ merely stared.

"I don't know what to say!" she exclaimed. "It's just that I forgot everything after I wrecked the truck."

Kemble looked at Russ. "A busy man like you, Martin," he said, "ought to be in bed early, anyway."

"I could be busier," Russ said, "if I had anything to work on."

Kemble winked at Janey. "Will I do?"

Janey said: "I don't know why we can't just all go on together."

Russ gave her a slow stare. He knew she had not forgotten. Yet he was not angry. "No use making it complicated," he said.

"If it was Harry's night, that's all there is to it." He paid for the drinks and left.

He did not see Janey for three days. He heard that Stevens's gang had cleaned up the last of the logs around the old site. The cat-and-arch were foraging higher, bringing back loads of recently cut timber.

Tuesday morning Stevens called him. "I heard from those friends of mine in Oregon," he said. "They'll take over my contract, all right. I'm leasing them my equipment. I expect Janey and I will leave by the end of the week."

"You're losing out on a good thing, Al," Russ argued. "Why not let me find a couple of fallers to replace the Kembles?"

"I guess not, Russ. Janey's kind of set on going."

Russ lit a cigarette. He threw it away and lit another. He went out onto the sawing floor. Then he saw Voss coming toward him.

"Want to see something?" he said.

They climbed a short flight of stairs. At the top, a dripping log lay ready for the deck saw. Voss put a tape on it. "Fourteen feet," he said.

Russ could feel the pressure building. At last something had importance besides Janey. He turned and went back down the stairs. Fourteen feet. The yards wanted nothing under sixteen-foot-lumber. Kemble had been cutting fourteen-foot logs up there ever since Stevens had told him to produce or get out. He was getting out, but he was having his joke first. The Lord only knew how many trees he had slaughtered.

Russ drove the twelve miles to the loading-out camp in twenty minutes.

Some impulse caused him to stop before the Stevens cabin. Janey came to the door, her hair pinned up and a dish-towel apron snugly about her hips. Russ walked up the path.

He could see the packing boxes in the middle of the room. "Don't tell me you can't take fifteen minutes for a ride," he said.

She hesitated. Russ reached around her and untied the apron. She let him take her to the car, but her chin was high. "I love masterful men," she said.

He sent the car on up the road. "I don't know which makes me madder," he said. "To have the Kembles buck my timber to fourteen feet, or to have you keep acting like a little theater ingénue."

Janey didn't answer. Russ stopped the car under a scarred fir. He took her hand, but she pulled it away. "Let's quit kidding each other," he said. "I know why you ran away when Voss was hurt. And I know Al isn't the thirty-day logger, but you are. It's no disgrace to be afraid of something, Janey."

She was breathing hard. She turned to open the door, but Russ held it shut. She whirled on him. "All right! It was my brother. I saw him fall and bounce like a doll. When I think about anything, I think about that. Because of that I'm a coward. Is that what you're trying to bring out?"

He clung to an elemental straw of logic. "I know you can't lick it by running away. If you'd only stop and look at it and stare it down. . . ." He held her hands. "Everybody's more or less afraid of the trees. Why do you think we pay a rigger fifteen dollars a day? Because there's nothing between his wife and widowhood but the belt he's hanging back on. But unless you carry that fear around with you, it's good for you. It keeps you on the jump."

The darkness went out of her eyes, but now there was nothing at all for him to see. "If you're going to be so technical, professor," she snapped, "I'm going to start cutting classes."

Russ swung back into the road. The Kemble business now seemed unimportant. "I'm sorry," he said. "It was none of my business, but I cared enough to make it mine."

It was another fifteen minutes to the falling camp. The first impression was of a battlefield littered with slain giants. He told Janey to wait in the car. It was rough climbing over the massive débris of logs and branches littering the slope. A little way up he stopped to listen. Someone was coming through a grove of young firs at his right. Whoever it was sounded as though he were running. Leo Kemble, Harry's brother, stumbled out of the trees. He saw Russ and stopped, his arms hanging.

"Russ," he said, "Harry . . . Harry's. . . ." He moved numbly toward him. "He's hung up. Spitted," he said. "He was topping a big one. The trunk split when the top went down."

Russ saw at once that Leo could help only by keeping out of the way. "My car's down below," he said. "Tell Janey Stevens to drive you back for help."

But as he ran on, he wondered how much one man could do to help Harry Kemble.

The tree stood at the edge of a clearing. About the base lay the branches Kemble had trimmed off in his ascent. From the ground, he appeared so small that the monstrous agony he was undergoing was inconceivable. But his moans were audible, and his voice, when he looked down and saw Russ, was a thin sob.

"Leo, you lousy, yellow. . . . Get your spikes, damn you!"

Russ saw that he supported his body by his elbows on the ragged table left by the topping. His safety belt hung loose. A gigantic splinter had snapped from the trunk and penetrated his body above the hip.

Russ found a jumble of equipment nearby. He had no illusions about being able to carry him down. He would have to be lowered by ropes. He lashed a block to a log. The other he slung over his shoulder, with the heavy coil of rope to make fast at the top. He was buckling the spikes on when he saw Janey.

He ran toward her, but she had already seen Kemble. He

caught her in his arms and turned her face from it. He said: "I told Leo you were to drive him down!"

Her voice was flimsy. "I thought . . . you might need me."

Need her! He needed her 100 miles from here. He was suddenly confronted by his own preaching. *If you'd only stop and stare it down.* . . . He looked at her a long time, then he led her to the lower block and put the rope in her hands. There was no denying that he needed someone on the ground . . . but Janey?

"If I can work him loose," he said, "I'll need you to lower him. Look at me, Janey . . . don't try it if you can't do it. It wouldn't help you, or Harry, either."

She was staring up at Kemble. "Russ . . . help him," she whispered.

As he ascended, bark fell in repeated showers. He went slowly, disciplining himself. He was conscious of the ground falling away. He was above the spires of the second growth and still climbing. Something bumped his head. He looked up at the hobnailed soles of Harry Kemble's boots.

He made his safety belt secure. Kemble's pale eyes did not know him. Russ talked as he made the block fast. "I'm going to lift you off that splinter. We'll have you down in five minutes."

Kemble spoke: "Don't move me!"

Russ brought the rope around his body and cinched it. He set his spikes firmly, standing beneath him, and put both hands on Kemble's hip. Suddenly his own knees began to shake. He had to stop and close his eyes. Then he lifted.

Kemble screamed. His body slacked and suddenly all his weight was in Russ's arms. Russ raised him until he saw the splinter, slender and tough as a rapier, come out of his hip. Then he gave Janey the signal to lower him. Kemble began to drop away. Russ was ready to hang on the rope himself if it began to run away; that would be no fun, either, but they'd get down somehow. He could see Janey's face turned up to him. He

173

watched her pay out the line hand over hand through the block.

He saw Kemble twist and swing, his head rolling.

But the hands down there did not falter, and, when Harry Kemble came slackly upon the earth, Janey ran to loosen the rope around his shoulders. Russ climbed down. He and Janey made no attempt to bring Kemble to consciousness. He seemed better off as it was.

Russ made Janey sit against the trees and gave her a drink from the canvas water bag. She sat there until the rescue gang arrived.

The doctors at Nevada City did not care to stake their reputations on Harry Kemble's recovery. But after a few days the opinion was ventured that he would live to buck a few more logs before he died.

One day Russ went up to see Janey.

He had heard about people conquering a fear just by being forced to contemplate it long enough. But sometimes those things backlashed.

They walked along the creek. She was quiet, but with a quietness like that of the water, betraying, by a race of moving glints, the swift cool heart of it. Suddenly he had to know. "I've still got a rain check for last Friday," he said. "How about that steak at the Clover Leaf?"

Janey took his arm. She said that would be grand. "But couldn't we go someplace where it's quiet?"

Russ stopped and turned her face up to him. "It's pretty quiet right here," he said. "I don't think the trees would tell on us."

She closed her eyes, waiting. "Let's see if they do," she said.

They didn't.

★ ★ ★ ★ ★

LONGHORNS ARE TOUGH

★ ★ ★ ★ ★

I

Sam Candler sat, gray-eyed, in the saddle outside the Kansas City loading pens and knew it had happened at last. The hot air was full of dust and misery. He looked at the strings of empties waiting on the sidings, at the pens that were a shifting, bawling, sweating flow of longhorn cattle. He saw wagons unloading tons of baled hay to feed these thousands of gaunt brown cattle. On the hills beyond the city he saw other thousands of steers.

After a long time he turned, but his rough, unshaven face, dark with sun color, possessed none of the satisfaction that might have shown on a man who has been proven a true prophet.

He said to Shorty Tylson: "There ain't room for a dogie yearling here. Ride back and tell the boys to flip for who rides herd tonight. The rest can come in and raise what hell they can without any money. I can't pay off until I see Miss Shelby and find out what's happened."

Shorty had his hat off. He wiped the back of his hand over the white, untanned strip of forehead above his hat brim. He was looking into the vast Kansas City stockyards with searching, anxious eyes.

"You think beef's took a tumble?" he asked.

"I think half the cattlemen in Texas and the territory are ruined," said Candler.

He rode through the sparse suburbs along the bluffs overlooking the tawny Missouri, cutting east into town. As he penetrated the city, the traffic thickened, drays and light buggies mingling with saddle horses in the wide streets of the business section. It was a big town and a clamorous one, filled with the ring of cattle dollars and trade dollars, battening on the salaries of railroad men and the reckless crews that took the steamboats up the Big Muddy. He passed hide and tallow factories and slaughterhouses, a brewery, a lumber and coal yard that had not been here when he hit town last year; closer in, livery stables, saloons, and stores dominated both sides of the streets.

He wondered what it would mean to the metropolis if, as he feared, the bottom had dropped out of the beef market. He wondered what would happen to Jo Shelby, Keith Wingate, and a score of others whose tally books were as large as the family Bible.

Sam Candler had told them three years ago that the bubble would burst. Longhorn prices could not keep climbing when every year saw the East producing more good shorthorn stock; someday the public would get tired of steaks that had to be bludgeoned into submission by weary teeth.

But crazy promotion schemes, reaching as far as Europe, put fantastic prices on the heads of these shaggy outlaws that a decade before had roamed the plains of Texas, wild and worthless. In spite of it, Sam Candler, who ran the Lightning Ranch for Jo Shelby while she spent the profits among Kansas City's bright lights, had tried to get her to give him a few hundred Herefords or Angus breeders.

"You should be an undertaker, Sam." Jo had laughed. "You're full of cheerful ideas. You just keep on bringing my longhorns up the trail and I'll sell them."

Candler had brought her 4,000 beeves this season; he wondered how much luck she would have in selling them.

Avoiding the saloons, Candler sought the bar of the Hoffman House, where it was said more cattle deals were made than at the stockyards. The atmosphere of the place was conducive to big business, with its low ceilings of paneled walnut to warm the blood of the shrewdest buyer, white-coated barmen, and a crystalline array of bottles and glasses to put the orneriest Texas cowman in an expansive mood.

Candler stood in the doorway, his eyes blinking from the tobacco smoke. He was tired, and his fatigue showed on him. 900 miles of mountain and prairie trails, of sand-stropped winds to roughen and toughen a man's skin, of brazen suns that leeched the last ounce of fat from his bones and put crow's-feet about his eyes, of black nights of storm and panic when death rode stirrup to stirrup with him—the marks of all these tests were on him, dragging a little at his shoulders, but leaving the hardness, the keenness of him exposed like an oil-stoned blade.

He crossed the room, a spare, tall man of thirty years in vest, shirt, and Levi's. He found a place at the bar between old Lane Horton and Keith Wingate.

He gave Horton his hand. "How long you been in?"

The cowman had a mustache like a sea cow and blue eyes that had lost the bright varnish of youth. "Since yesterday," he said, and that was all.

"How's beef sellin'?"

Horton regarded him sharply, as if suspecting sarcasm, looked at the spittoon, then, and patronized it with care. "It ain't."

"Not selling. What's the matter?"

A cattle buyer named Sayman glared at him across his beer. His face was flushed with drinking, and he looked worn down with telling a hundred cattlemen he did not want their beef.

"It seems like some meat packer in Chicago with false teeth ran across a shorthorn steak," he said dryly. "He found he could eat it without boiling it in brine for three days, hammering it with an eight-pound maul, and cutting it in pieces a half inch square. Now they're all hollering for Hereford and Angus and

Durham. If you're selling longhorns, try the Indian reservations."

Keith Wingate bit off the end of a twisted New Orleans cigar and spat the brown nubbin on the floor. "It looks like your cue to say . . . 'I told you so,' " he remarked.

Wingate was another who ran his cattle ranch from a distance. Like Jo Shelby, he had never seen it, having come by it when a long-looping pioneer grandfather got in the way of a Mescalero arrow. Wingate was husky and blond and possessed of a drawling assurance. He wore his sideburns down to the angle of his jaw and kept an insolent little sandy mustache on his lip. In his tailored suit, that flattered the wide swing of his shoulders, he had more grace and polish than Sam Candler could have taken on in 100 years of being barbered and tailored.

Sam gave him a quick, level stare. "All I do is work twenty-four hours a day raising these brutes. Do you think I feel like crowing because I've cussed them a thousand miles up the trail and now find I can't sell them?" He waited until Wingate's eyes dropped, and then asked: "What's happened to the market?"

"None of the packers will set a price until they hear from the East," Wingate growled. "We hear a hundred boat loads of cattle came over from England last summer. Nobody knows how it's going to affect longhorn beef. But until they do, they aren't buying."

"The town's dead," Horton said with disgust. "Slaughter-houses closed, saloons empty, hide an' taller men going broke without any hide an' taller to handle. Railroad men are moochin' drinks until the Chicago packers start wiring for beef."

To Sayman, Sam Candler said: "What are you paying for shorthorns?"

"There's only been one herd of them in. That Montana rancher drew fifty-five a head. A man could get sixty now." He smiled. "But you ain't going to fool me by sawing the horns off those *ladinos* of yours, cowboy. It takes more than short horns to make a Hereford."

"Mine have got more than short horns," Candler said quietly. "Like to ride out this afternoon and take a look at them?"

Sayman stared at him, and Keith Wingate's eyes snapped to the cowman's dark, uninformative face. The whole room was instantly at attention.

"Are you making a joke?" Sayman asked. "I thought you said you brought in longhorns."

"I did . . . for Miss Shelby. I've got a hundred and fifty of my own white-faces."

Lane Horton scowled at him, still disbelieving. "Where'd you run into any Herefords?" he demanded.

"Had 'em four years," the Lightning foreman told him and the room. "An Englishman came in one day and thought he was going to run cattle. He found out you can't pasture a herd on ten acres, like in England, and he thought he was getting out cheap when he sold to me for twenty-five hundred. Nobody else would touch them. There was a theory goin' around that shorthorns weren't strong enough to tough it out on salt bush and grama. But the only thing I've found about them that ain't tough is their meat. If you'd like to look at them, Sayman, meet me here at two. I'll be taking out some other buyers."

Sayman's pudgy hand produced a checkbook by a sort of legerdemain, and he held it up like a magic wand. "Sixty a head, sight unseen!" he exclaimed. "Bartender . . . pen and ink!"

Wingate raised his hand. "I'll pay you sixty-five for all but the steers," he cut in sharply.

Candler spoke to him without raising his voice, and through the growing murmur Wingate heard him and his face flushed: "You've got your guts, Wingate. I wouldn't see a cow of mine wearing your brand if I was starving."

Wingate murmured: "You still feel that way, do you?" His tone was too casual; his eyes were talking with Candler's, and they were sullen with a small fear.

"You're still running the same kind of an outfit, ain't you?"

Wingate put his whiskey glass to his lips and did not answer. He finished the drink and left, with Candler still the hub of excited talk.

II

Candler got out as soon as he could, promising only to let the meat buyer bid against the other packers' reps that afternoon. He rode down a quiet street of tree-shaded residences.

His jaw muscles tightened when he saw Wingate's horse before Jo Shelby's home. Jo lived here with a widowed aunt, enjoying the profits of a hard, tough business without ever knowing a day's hardship. Sam Candler, who had fought and sweated beside old Dirty Shirt Shelby, and knew the price he had paid to bind the Lightning Ranch into a workable unit, bitterly resented that.

Jo and Wingate were in earnest conversation on the porch when Candler dismounted and dropped his reins over the white picket fence. Jo met him at the top step, giving him a hand that was firm and warm.

"I'm glad to see you, Sam," she said. "I saw a herd come in this morning, and I hoped it would be yours. How is the ranch?"

"Prospering," replied Candler. "K.C. seems a little quiet this year."

He tried to read in her face how much Wingate had told her, but if other things had changed about Jo Shelby in the past year, one thing had not, and that was the quiet self-confidence, the cool impersonality that her emotions wore. She seemed taller, more mature of figure. She was wearing her dark hair differently, in little frills and ringlets, and it made her face as young and alive as it had seemed that first day Sam had seen her, when he had come up from the territory with her grandfather, five years past and more.

"Kansas City is very quiet, indeed," Jo said. And then, suddenly: "What are we going to do with all those steers, Sam? How are we going to get our money out of them?"

"There's the problem," said Candler. He sat on the porch railing beside Keith Wingate, shaking dry flakes of tawny tobacco into a troughed paper.

"You aren't very helpful." Jo spoke shortly; color was coming to the soft hollows of her cheeks. It was the first time she had shown fear in Candler's remembrance, but fear it was—the same terror that had most of the cattlemen west of the Mississippi anxiously consulting their bankers.

"I tried to be helpful last year. I think you suggested that I take up embalming if I had to go around hanging crêpe."

Jo's hand made a quick, impulsive motion. "I was wrong. I'm not ashamed to admit it. But it doesn't make the problem any easier to solve to remind me of it. We've got to sell those steers!"

Sam Candler gave the cigarette his frowning attention, coddling it into shape and licking the edge of the brown paper. She watched him, biting her lips, waiting for him to speak. As he put a match to the tobacco, his eyes raised to hers, but still he had nothing to say.

In exasperation, Jo turned angrily and went a few steps to lean by one hand on the rail beside Keith Wingate.

Candler spoke finally. "Longhorns are finished. The price ain't coming up. Did you tell her I've got my own herd of whitefaces, Wingate?"

Across his square shoulder Candler saw the answer in her face. Anger slid like a hot blade into him when he heard her say in icy politeness: "Whose grass did you fatten them on, Sam?"

"On my own," he snapped. "I bought the Englishman out

entire. But I could have been raising cattle on the Lightning for five years, and you'd never have known it. I could have rustled you blind and you'd still have been up here among your good-time friends while the place went broke. If you'd given me any co-operation these last couple of years, I could have kept the props under it."

"I suppose I should have come down and managed it myself?"

"If you wanted to see it run right."

"Suppose I come down and start now?"

Candler didn't know whether she was serious or not. Her blue eyes were a snapping black and every mark of temper was on her.

"If you could raise five or six thousand to put into shorthorn breeders, maybe it would do some good," he said. "But I doubt that you could."

"Would you sell me your own herd cattle on credit?"

"Don't be foolish, Jo!" Wingate turned his head to look at her with angry impatience. "He'd hold you up. In a year or so he'd own the place."

Looking around him, Jo said again: "Would you sell?"

"How much?" Candler said it more to test her; if she were bluffing, this would face her down. "The ones I brought up are mostly steers, but I've got four hundred herd animals still down there that I'd sell . . . if the price was right. . . ."

"Sixty dollars."

"For sixty-five I might. Nothing down, five years to pay, and I keep my job till it's paid off."

Jo Shelby came around Wingate and put out her hand. "Then it's a deal. You've got an exaggerated idea of how useless I am and how infallible you are. I'm going back with you. Maybe we'll both get our eyes opened up . . . or perhaps just one of us."

Keith Wingate was on his feet and watching them shake

hands. He said—"Good Lord, Jo!"—but the girl faced him quickly with a brittle, challenging smile.

"Why don't you come along, Keith? Your ranch could stand some personal supervision."

"That's not a lie," remarked Candler with meaning.

Wingate was silent an instant, and then he shrugged. "Well, why not? We'll go down together."

But Candler quickly clouded the sparkle that came to Jo's eyes. "I don't know how good it would look for you and me to blow into Ladron with a Wingate. Dirty Shirt and this gent's granddaddy, Brig Wingate, always had their coup sticks notched for each other, and it's sort of been a tradition that their ramrods did the same after they were gone. Gil Kenesaw and I have tried to keep the idea intact."

"That's childishness." Jo sniffed. "I know my grandfather was always fighting down there, but I hardly think Keith and I will feel obliged to carry the feud on any longer."

"That," said Sam Candler, "is because you never had to fight for your bread and butter. If Wingate wants to tell his cow-stealin', brand-blottin' ramrod, Gil Kenesaw, to take a long *pasear* yonderly, we can end it right now. But there's the matter of Cedar Lodge Springs and the salt beds. No Antlers man has ever been able to savvy that those wore a Lightning brand. There's been some shootings over them and plenty of rustling, and it's still going on."

Jo snapped: "Then it's time it stopped. If you're satisfied with the price, Sam, I'll meet you at my lawyer's tomorrow and we'll draw it up."

"See here, Jo!" Keith Wingate's exclamation came with a burst of exasperation. "Hasn't it occurred to you that sixty-five dollars is a lot to pay for your own cattle?"

The remark fell in a space of silence like a bright blade shimmering in a plank floor. Sam Candler threw his cigarette into the yard.

"That's too subtle for my sun-baked brains," he said. "Make it plainer." He was leaning against a puncheon of the porch, but there was something so bowstring tight about him that Wingate held his answer for one moment while he looked at him.

"I mean," he said, "that we have no way of knowing whether you've lied about how you came by these cattle. For all Jo knows, you may have sold some of her own steers to buy them."

Candler's fist hit his jaw with a sound like a cleaver biting a joint of beef. Lifted off his feet by the force of the blow, Wingate crashed against the scroll-worked railing, carrying a length of it with him as he fell from the porch. A shrub caught him and supported his body grotesquely. To Candler, there was something eminently satisfying in the picture; a man lost a lot of elegance in a pose like that, even if his sideburns were the longest in town.

Sam realized now that Jo had screamed. As white as chalk, she brought her gaze from Wingate back to Candler.

"You've killed him!" she gasped.

"Maybe," said Sam. "But I'll wager that a bucket of water will work a resurrection. You might try it." He went down the steps and loaded the man's body back to the porch. Wingate was groaning softly.

"As long as you don't ring him in as a pardner, the deal is still all right with me," he remarked. "I'll see you at the lawyer's."

To his mild surprise, Jo Shelby held to the bargain.

In the lawyer's office, Sam Candler read the contract she had had the man draw up. It was so riveted with legality that apparently nothing could break it. Candler was to receive his money in five equal installments, due yearly. He was to remain as foreman of the Lightning Ranch until the period was up. But he could not divide his time by working any ranch of his own; thus he knew that it was sink or swim with the Lightning.

Yet this was no hardship. The Lightning had been home range for so long that he could not imagine it going into any hands but those of a Shelby, and even if the present owner was a pale excuse for a Shelby, Sam Candler would at least make an honest fight for the memory of a tough, game old war horse whose last words to Sam had been of the ranch.

III

Those six weeks she rode a chuck wagon behind a span of mules worked a hard change in the pretty, headstrong girl who had sworn to show Sam Candler she was as game and as able to run a ranch as he. For companionship she had only grumpy old Rocky Pike, on whose tough hide her smiles and attempts at friendliness made not the smallest dent. She felt her inadequacy still more when she attempted to help with the cooking. Rocky tolerated her for a few days and finally let her know that he had managed alone for thirty years and could still struggle along.

Keith Wingate had left three days before the Lightning crew, and from that day until they reached Ladron she did not see him again.

A price of $15 had been set finally on longhorn beef, and every cattleman in town had sold on the spot. Jo had sold out and paid the hands, and two days later the Lightning crew had left town.

After the plains swallowed them, the cowboys took to spinning hair-raising windies around the supper fires, yarns that had the odor of burning flesh in massacred wagon trains, the war gobbles of raiding Arapahoes. For weeks they saw no one but an occasional horseman or a news-hungry trader at some lonely crossing.

Fear came into Jo Shelby's heart, and loneliness, and a great longing to be back at home. And as these feelings cut deeper, she came to hate the man who had brought her out here. She didn't see much of Sam Candler, but when he watched her over a cigarette or a cup of coffee, there was mockery in his eyes. He could see into the scared heart of her, and he knew she would quit now if she possibly could.

But because she could not, and because her hatred for Candler was such, she put on an armor of boredom, of scorn for these vast reaches of prairie the cowboys seemed to love, for the blue, towering mountains their eyes reverenced as they drew closer to them.

The complexion she had guarded with a silk parasol toughened and became tawny. Into the corners of her blue eyes two small lines pinched, gift of a sun that, even if fading to a pale wintry yellow, was bright as a new coin. In the mountains there were cold autumn nights to keep her shivering under her blankets, lusty streams to ford that left her weak for an hour after the perilous crossing had been made.

On a bitterly cold December morning, Sam Candler pulled rein on a wind-combed ridge. He said in a casual tone: "This is it, lady."

Jo, in surprise, stood up on the wagon and looked across the valley. It was deep and wide, cut by a half dozen chains of low hills and barricaded far to the west by a great, saddle-shaped mountain, blue-gray in the distance. The grass was deep and frost-yellow, and the clean odor of it filled her lungs. She could see cattle, thousands of them. Far off, at the fork of a creek, she discerned a town.

"How much of it is Lightning?" she asked.

"Everything south of the town, between the mountain ranges, and about ten miles out into the plains. Wingate's range runs north of town, and my iron lies in between."

He swung his pony, not giving her time to take it all in. They descended the hump and came to a small, dry lake whose floor was dirty gray salt. Here Candler sat very still in the saddle, and Shorty Tylson pulled up beside him. She heard the foreman swear.

"That bronc'-brained fool! He's let a hundred wagons haul salt out of here if he's let one."

"I was afraid of it," muttered Shorty. "Al Coates and Gil Kenesaw were always too thick. I wonder how much he charged per wagon."

Sam Candler looked at the marks of scores of wagon wheels, at the shallow trenches from which the salt had been shoveled. No Antlers wagon had hauled salt from here in ten years, not since Dirty Shirt Shelby had found Brig Wingate selling the salt he let him take out for his cattle. Since then the salt beds had been No Man's Land for Wingate cowboys.

"Al Coates hasn't made enough out of it to make it worthwhile to him," Candler said. "I can promise that."

They rode on. In a round meadow bordered by gray-green piñons and black oaks, Candler flushed a bunch of cattle out of a willow brake. The first thing he noticed was that they were his own shorthorns, and his ears went red as he felt Jo's eyes on him. Then he saw that only part of them were Herefords; the rest were longhorns.

When the wagon drew up, Jo could see that something was wrong. She called to him: "What's the matter?"

Pike came off the seat, staring.

"What's wrong?" Jo called again, and now alarm was in her voice.

Sam Candler turned in the saddle, his cheeks flat and his eyes like dead coals. "This is why us and the Wingates have never got along," he said. "We've been set back a full year. The man I left in charge let Gil Kenesaw throw my shorthorns in

189

with your cutbacks. The spring drop won't be worth trailing to K.C."

Where a crystal brook brawled down a cañon through a motte of oaks, Dirty Shirt Shelby had built a spring house of round, washed boulders in which to keep the quarters of beef, tubs of butter, and hams and bacons that a full bunkhouse required. Around this he had Mexican laborers build him barns and a smithy, a labyrinth of split-rail corrals, and a vast, echoing house of whitewashed adobe in which he had lived alone, a sad-eyed old grizzly who never took another mate after his first died.

Beneath the windows, at front, back, and side of the U-shaped fortress, he had had rifle loops fashioned. Hostile Indians had been regular visitors in the late 1850s, and a man never knew what kind of neighbors he might draw. Dirty Shirt Shelby had never regretted those loopholes.

There was a look of emptiness about the ranch as they rode in, but Candler's shout brought three cowpunchers from the bunkhouse. They came up with grins and handshakes, but one look into the ramrod's face sobered them.

"Where's Coates?" he demanded.

"Al?" Blond Cotton Riley frowned. "He rode into town last night."

"Have you men been shooting craps in there ever since I left?" Candler snapped out.

Their soberness became apprehension, and Jo Shelby read in their faces that Candler's anger was not a pleasant thing.

"What's wrong, boss?" Cotton asked.

"Did you know the salt beds have been raided?"

Riley rubbed his nose. "Them danged Antlers riders jumped it a month ago."

"I suppose it's news that my Seven Spot cows are in with the longhorns?"

"Can't be! I was over there a week ago. Your cows were doing fine and a good two miles inside your range."

Candler looked steadily at him, and he said: "I'll know next spring whether you're lyin' to me, Cotton. If they only got in that late, there can't be any harm done. Even the late breeders are through by now. But if next spring's calves have longer horns than their mammies, cowboy, there's going to be a general dehorning around here."

Cotton raised his right hand fervently. "Stack o' Bibles, boss!"

Candler, dismounting, spoke to Rocky Pike. "Shake up some chow. Feed the boys good, because they're going out on roundup today. I want every shorthorn cut out and thrown on the south forty. After that, we'll talk about resting."

Jo Shelby went into the house. Her nose rebelled at the ancient odors filling the place. Obviously it had known neither broom nor occupant since her grandfather's death. She looked about her, at the red furniture fashioned from native juniper, at the musty lynx and bear hides nailed to the wall, at the ponderous beams supporting a ceiling of cottonwood-branch riprapping. There was, she thought, some hope of making the place livable, if every stick of furniture were moved out and the place swept, scrubbed, and fumigated. She thought of herself living here, the only woman on the place, and the thought appalled her.

When she went out onto the wide-puncheoned porch, Sam Candler had saddled another pony and was just putting his toe into the stirrup. "For heaven's sake!" she called. "Now where?"

Candler buttoned his blue denim jumper against the cold wind rising through the trees. "To town," he said, "to find Al Coates."

He crossed the bridge and followed the creek, lean and tall in the saddle, his Stetson pulled low on his face and his shoulders hunched.

Those six words of his had brought all the cold of the winter about her heart. She had seen what he would do when a man spoke out of turn; it was not comforting to think of what he would do when he had actually been betrayed.

There was something about Sam Candler that frightened her. In anger he was cold and deadly; he was intolerant of inefficiency and deception. Yet she had seen him joshing with the boys when night drew its dark cloak about the camp and the day's responsibilities were soothed by the fire's warm fingers. She knew they liked and respected him, that they relied on him to meet any emergency quickly and intelligently.

To her, Candler was a riddle. But women have long had a way of solving such riddles, and Jo smiled faintly as his hoof beats faded down the cañon.

Candler crossed the bridge in the late afternoon and rode into Ladron. The town was in its drab winter tweeds, the chinaberries leafless, and only a few tattered leaves rattling against the branches of the big cottonwood in front of the bank.

Coming back to Ladron was always pleasant, for he liked the unhurried pace of the Spanish-American town; it was good to see the misshapen adobe huts of the Mexican quarter and the picket-fenced American homes, and, farther along, the brown wooden awnings of the stores overhanging the boardwalks.

But none of these warmed his gray eyes this afternoon. As he dismounted before the saloon, he heard a man's voice almost in warning—"There's Sam Candler!"—and what activity there had been in the street ceased. He made a loop with his reins about the tooth-scarred rack, and paused before entering to pull the buckskin glove off his left hand. He tucked it under his belt, using this same motion to slip his Peacemaker forward.

He went inside, to stand with his lanky form sketched in long strokes against the slatted doors. A man said: "You're late, Sam.

I've been back a week."

In the dusk he saw Lane Horton at the bar. There were others in the saloon, too, but not Keith Wingate, Gil Kenesaw, or Al Coates.

"You weren't traveling with a woman," Candler said grimly, and the men laughed.

Candler had a beer with them. Sheriff Dunk Hale was there, a whiskey-fancying old lawman with a ready joke and an unready gun. In ten years of policing Ladron, Hale had had many sleepless nights when the Antlers-Lightning feud seemed about to flare high, but somehow the cocked gun was never fired, and Hale still walked his tight wire.

"I hear you're runnin' fillies now," the sheriff said with a wink at Horton.

Candler wiped his mouth. "Or maybe a filly will be running me," he remarked. Then, in the same tone he asked: "Where's Al Coates?"

"Coates?" Hale made his expression too blank. "Why, I reckon . . . ain't he down at the livery barn, Lane?"

Horton nodded. Candler flipped a coin to the bar, and the cowman added: "With Wingate and Kenesaw."

"That's fine," Sam Candler said. "I have something I want them all to hear."

He was almost to the door when Dunk Hale called hurriedly: "Now, wait a minute, feller! I don't want no trouble . . . no gun trouble, you understand?"

"If there's gun trouble, I won't start it."

Tut Akers's barn was down a block and over a block, but Candler walked it, finding the exercise relaxing. He was sure, when he turned the corner, that he saw four men in front of the barn, but when he entered the yard there were only Keith Wingate and his foreman sitting on the edge of a flat bed, and Tut Akers leaning against a wheel, his fingers busy with a piece of broken harness and some copper wire.

Akers looked up quickly, a florid-jowled, black-haired man. He said: "Glad to see you back, Sam."

"I guess everybody is," Candler remarked. "Keeping busy, Kenesaw?"

Kenesaw was a Swede, his skin fair and his eyebrows blond, and he was built on the heavy-muscled, big-boned structure of his race. He wore a red plaid shirt and denims that were soft with wear. His fists and his face had the small white scars of a man who has done some fighting, and his jaw was massive, his nose flat.

"Busy enough," Kenesaw said. "How's K.C.?"

Candler's lips smiled a little. "Pretty dull. Eh, Wingate?"

Wingate had changed; he was browner, harder-looking, and his face was sullen.

"What's on your mind?" he said shortly.

"Where's Al Coates?"

"Over at the ranch, I guess."

"Then he's been ridin' fast. Because I saw him standing right here a minute ago." Candler turned and strode toward the barn.

"I wouldn't go in there!" Kenesaw warned.

"Why not?"

Kenesaw was frank. "Because Al's in there. And he ain't going to take any fist whipping from you."

Candler went in and stood in the semidarkness, tasting the warm fragrance of horse sweat and dry hay and leather; the yard behind him was in bright sunlight, and he put himself beyond the edge of the wide doors. He made out the long line of horse stalls lining the left-hand wall, saw the mountainous bulk of a mound of bailed hay on his right, and farther down a jumble of traps and buggies, saddle gear hung against the wall. And suddenly, although he could not see Coates, he heard his breathing very close, above the champing of a horse in a near stall.

IV

Candler said tightly: "You might as well step out, Coates, because you're going to get it if I have to follow you all over New Mexico."

"No, I ain't." Coates's voice had a snarl in it, the sharp backbone of panic. "You've been kingpin hereabouts a long time, but you ain't settin' fist to me. Get out!"

Candler could see him now, standing beside a roof support, a long, warped figure wearing a flat-crowned Stetson. His imagination filled in the hollow cheeks and the chin that was like a saddle horn, the sunken eyes, the twisted, thin lips dominated by a nose curved like a saber.

"So you sold me out," he said. "I trusted you to keep the Antlers in line, and all the time you were swillin' their whiskey and giving them the run of the place. And you thought you could get away with it!"

"Don't try to pin what's happened on me," Coates retorted. "You can't hog all the water and grass in sight and not have a few kicks aimed at your britches. I've quit the Lightning. And I'm taking nothing from you."

Candler started toward him. "You're going to take the worst whipping I ever gave a man."

Coates straightened; Candler saw the sparkle of blue gun steel, and for the first time he knew the ex-range boss held a gun in his hand.

"Do you want a slug in your belly?" Al Coates snarled.

Candler halted. "I'm warning you, Coates . . . put it away."

The cowpuncher's words came with a scrape across the silence: "When I see you ride out of town, I'll put it away. Until I do. . . ."

Sam Candler spoke softly. "Then I'll have to take it away." He started toward him once more. Without warning, Al Coates fired.

The shock of it—the single blast of gases exploding against his eardrums, the orange burst of flame blinding him—hit Candler like a fist, and his stomach muscles snapped taut. He had not rated Coates with enough guts to do it, and so for an instant he stood rigidly, feeling a sledge-hammer blow against his hip.

He saw Coates moving backward, as if to run out the rear door. Candler's fingers caught under the smooth butt of his .45 and he brought it out of the holster with a jerk, leveling it even with his belt and snapping his thumb down across the spur.

He could feel the concussion against his eyeballs. He heard Al Coates gasp. He stepped quickly behind the stanchion but it was a needless precaution. The lanky gunman was down, his cheek pressed against the hard dirt floor and one arm crumpled under him.

The sunlight blinded Candler, but he saw Wingate and Kenesaw and the stable man standing near the door and heard others running from the main street.

"He fired first," he said. "You heard the shots."

No man spoke. Candler pressed a hand against his hip. The heavy gun belt was ripped and blood was warm and sticky against his palm. Slowly he walked to the street.

Fat Sheriff Hale met him at the corner. He was panting and excited. "What in hell!" he gasped. "What in hell!"

Candler said dryly: "Al Coates coyoted. He pulled a gun on me, wounded me, and forced me to shoot him."

"Is . . . is he dead?"

"I think so. I'm going up to Doc's, Hale, and get patched up. I'll leave my written version of it with him."

"You'd better stay in town, mister," Hale expostulated.

"There'll be an investigation."

"Fine. You can find me at Cedar Lodge Springs if you want me. But don't go swearing out any warrants, because I'll tear them up and throw them in your face."

Al Coates's bullet had pulled a long gash open in Candler's side, but the wound, if disabling, was not deep, and the doctor cleaned it thoroughly and taped it so tightly that he could hardly breathe. While he lay face down on the pine operating table, the realization came into him for the first time that he had killed a man. It left a feeling of queasiness in him, and brought home the certainty that anything could happen now. First blood lay, red and ominous, across the valley. And he had spilled it.

If he had been more or less sure of his course up to this point, the trail ahead had suddenly become unpredictable. How Wingate would take the killing, what answer Gil Kenesaw would choose to make, were impossible to guess. But damned bad trouble was brewing.

The ride home left him too weary to join the roundup crew at Cedar Lodge Springs. He slept alone in the bunkhouse that night.

His breakfast of fried potatoes, ham, and a pot of coffee was sizzling on Rocky's cranky cook stove when Jo Shelby came into the kitchen next morning. To his surprise she wore a leather riding skirt and a warm woolen shirt, and there was high color in her cheeks. She pulled off fringed gauntlets and threw them on a chair.

The ache in Candler's side made his voice testy. "Don't tell me you've been out already."

"Since sunup." Her eyes were bright and much of her stiffness toward him had relaxed. "I rode to the top of a ridge and watched the sunlight pour into the valley. I think I'll be able to get used to this country, Sam. Are the mornings all like this?"

"Most of 'em," Candler grunted. "When they really look pretty is after you've been jinglin' horses or huntin' a cow thief all night and you're half froze and hungry enough to eat pine bark. Then you can appreciate a little sunlight."

They ate on the work table in the kitchen, Candler stiff and silent. He was not particularly surprised to hear hoofs drum across the bridge and stop before the house. He went to the door and watched Bart Gillett, Kenesaw's top-hand bronco-stomper, come toward the house. He stepped outside.

Gillett wore a heavy sheepskin saddle coat and goatskin chaps, and his blunt Irish features were red with cold. Every muscle of Candler's body was in sharp vigilance. But the other man stepped along too briskly to be planning any gun play, and he did not remove his gloves.

He handed Candler a folded paper. "Hale wants you in town on the Fifteenth," he said. "Coates done quit."

Candler glanced at the document. "What's he planning?"

Gillett, who was short and chunky and tough as bull hide, pulled a sack of tobacco from his pocket and took off one glove. "Coroner's inquest," he told him. "It's a sort of formality when somebody's died real sudden."

Jo spoke sharply, close behind Sam. "Coates is dead?"

There was a moment's awkwardness, with the Antlers man glancing at the girl, and then at Candler.

Sam said without looking back: "Al Coates tried to kill me. It was his tough luck that he didn't shoot straight, because I did."

"You killed him . . . over my cattle!" The thought made her stand very straight, white as paper.

"Over *our* cattle," he reminded her. "But Coates dealt the cards himself. It was his game, and, when he started dealing lead at me, I had to go to bat with him." He said to Gillett: "Tell him I'll be in. Is that all you wanted?"

"No. I'm repping for Wingate on this roundup you're pulling

off. I'm ready to ride whenever you are."

Candler nodded. It was not a thing he could refuse, because to deny any neighboring rancher the right to witness a roundup was generally accepted as an admission that a good percentage of your weanlings needed the kind of brands that are slapped on in the big dark of the moon.

When he went in for his hat, Jo Shelby was gone.

They worked the Cedar Lodge Springs section for two days, finding most of Candler's 400 shorthorns in the jumbled cañons and rough brakes. It was mountainous country that tried a man's skill and courage. The roundup crew rode rough, sure-footed ponies with heavy stock saddles cinched fore and aft; stout breast rigs anchored the tree still more firmly against the shock of fair-grounding a fighting bull.

The mouth of Dutchman's Draw provided a natural corral where a few cowpunchers could hold the cattle. They finished combing the timber the second day, and on the third morning branding of the shorthorns and the few maverick longhorns commenced.

At a half dozen fires, men kept the branding irons hot while other cowpunchers cut out the steers, threw them, and burned the brand into the hairy red hide until the smoking flesh was black as a burned steak. In the midst of all this dust, cow bawling, and smoke Sam Candler stood with his red tally book, noting down the brands as they were called to him.

He was standing like that when Shorty Tylson came up to him. There was a curiously strained look on Tylson's homely, freckled face that caused the foreman to ask sharply: "What's wrong?"

Shorty rubbed his chin. "Better take a look at this shorthorn, boss."

Candler walked over to where Bart Gillett and a cowpuncher

had a big herd bull three-footed near an ironwood fire. Gillett was standing with his Stetson shoved back, frowning down at the bull. The cowboy was gingerly touching the animal's free leg.

Fear came suddenly into Sam Candler's heart; the stunning, breathless dread of something a man cannot fight. Squatting on his heels, he rubbed his hand over the rough, hairy foreleg. He felt the hard lumps under the surface of the terribly swollen leg; he heard the sharp crackling of gas pockets in the tissue.

He held the bull's mouth open and glanced in, and saw how the tongue and cheeks were swollen and red with small festered spots on the skin. When he looked up, Bart Gillett was watching him closely.

"What would you call it?" Gillett asked.

Candler looked at Shorty, seeing in his red face the same heart-sunk desperation he himself was feeling.

He said quietly: "I suppose you'd call it blackleg."

Blackleg! The word sobered every man in the corral. Some had had experience with blackleg epidemics; the rest had heard grisly stories about it.

There was a Texas cattleman years back who had started up the trail with a few steers in his herd suffering from the dread disease. By the time he reached Kansas his whole herd was gone. Everywhere his cattle had trod other cases sprang up. Vets tried to treat hundred of cows without saving a single one. Whole sections were turned into a shambles of dead cattle littering the ground.

When it was known that the disease was impossible to treat, states and territories passed laws compelling any rancher who discovered blackleg to kill every infected cow and bury it. In that way the disease had been held under control with some success.

It was accepted, now, that a cowman must kill every infected animal as soon as it was discovered, and that his entire herd should be quarantined until it was learned whether any more cases would spring up.

Leaving the bull tied on the ground, Candler went to inspect the other roped animals. No other cases were found. He had the infected bull dragged away and put a .45 slug through its head. Then he turned to Shorty.

"I want the cows we've already branded brought back. We'll inspect the rest as we go through them. I can't corral feed them all up here, so we'll give them the run of the range within a couple of miles. That may keep it from going through the herd, too."

When he returned to the corral, Bart Gillett was gone. But during the rest of that grueling day Gillett's sardonic presence was over the draw. Sam Candler, feeling despair run like a leaden pulse through him, saw seven more cattle dragged off to be shot, and five of them were shorthorns.

He knew that of all the enemies he had fought, this was the first he really feared. Here, he thought, was an enemy he could not fight; here was a black terror that could ruin a man in a week.

At sundown Gillett returned with Keith Wingate, Gil Kenesaw, and Sheriff Dunk Hale.

Hale was full of whiskey and belligerence. As he rode into the pen, Candler closed the tally book and slipped it into his jumper pocket. Hale spoke without dismounting, liking the sense of dominance it gave him.

"I guess you know what I'm here for," he said heavily, meaningly.

Candler said: "Sure. To do a little blowing. I know what I've got to do."

"I'll tell you, in case you've got any doubts. You're going to kill every cow branded today and every other one that was in

201

the corral with them infected steers. And you're going to bury
them in quicklime."

Keith Wingate had dismounted, and he was taking up slack
in the latigo as if this grim business was of small concern to
him. "How many of your shorthorns were up here?" he asked.

"All of them," Candler said.

Wingate shook his head. "That's going to make it hard on
Jo."

If they had expected to find Candler ready to be dictated to,
he surprised them. "Maybe it is, maybe it isn't. I'm holding all
the cattle right in this section, but I'm not killing any that aren't
infected. That way I'll be playing fair with the surrounding
ranchers as well as myself."

"The hell you are!" Kenesaw snapped. "What happens if one
of these critters wanders across the hump onto our range?"

"I'll see that none of them does."

"That's not good enough," Wingate said shortly. "The sheriff
was talking for every man in Ladron when he said you've got to
get rid of those cattle. Our cattle are worth little enough alive,
without having a plague wipe them out."

Hale, bolstered by the support of numbers, softened a little.
"It's tough, Sam. You know I don't wish you any hard luck. But
I've got my responsibility to the rest."

Candler's eyes were gray sleet, and he stood hip-shot, his
hands tucked flat under his belt.

"What's your cut out of this?" he asked the sheriff.

The red, angry blood pumped into Hale's face.

Candler went on. "They've either hired or badgered you into
throwing the book at me." He looked at Hale with anger in his
dark face and in the rising force of his voice, and then he looked
at Wingate and Kenesaw. "You couldn't have had things more
your way if you had God and the twelve apostles on your side.
But you're crowding your luck too far if you think you can rub

my nose in the dirt. I'll keep my cattle penned up till I know whether or not I can control the plague. If I see it's getting out of hand, I'll do what's fair to the rest of you. But, Sheriff, if you or anybody else comes up with a load of quicklime, he'll ride out with blue whistlers nippin' his tail."

Hale was wordless, glancing at Kenesaw, and the Antlers foreman gave an answer as short and hard as Candler's.

"We'll give you one week, Candler, to make up your mind. If you haven't killed them by then, we'll be up and do it for you."

"All right," Sam said quietly, knowing he had won a point. "But bring enough quicklime to take care of some extra carcasses. There may be some."

V

Keith Wingate left Kenesaw and the sheriff at a trail fork and rode over to the Lightning headquarters. He saw a Lightning pony in the dark corral and guessed correctly that one of the cowpunchers had been sent back to tell Jo Shelby what had happened. There were lamps burning in the vast front room of the adobe building.

Jo let him in, looking infinitely weary. Wingate took her hands and said with sincerity: "I'm sorry, Jo. Terribly sorry."

Jo shook her head, biting her lip, and for a moment they sat in silence by a ponderous juniper table on which a lamp with a stained-glass shade burned high.

"What is going to happen?" she asked him.

Wingate's long body slumped in a cowhide arm chair, his legs extended. He scowled at his boots. "It seems to be in Candler's hands," he remarked. "Sheriff Hale told him all the cows in the day herd must be slaughtered. Candler's refused."

Across the table, Jo regarded his clean-cut profile with shock. "But aren't all the Herefords in the day herd?"

"All of them. It's hard, Jo. It's tragic for you. But Hale is only doing what he must . . . what the cowmen of Ladron insist that he do. Otherwise, this whole range could be wiped clean."

After a moment Jo asked: "What does Candler intend to do?"

"We can guess. Kenesaw gave him a week to kill the cattle, promising we'd come to do it for him if he hadn't slaughtered them by then. Candler threatens to resist with force."

Jo said nothing; Keith Wingate said suddenly, with truculence: "Why don't you fire the man, Jo? He'll draw you into the bloodiest range war the territory has ever seen. And the Lightning will be in the wrong."

"Will it, Keith?" Jo asked, and her voice carried both a puzzled and an impatient note.

"Reason it out for yourself," snapped Wingate. "Because of one man's selfishness a whole range will be ruined."

"But even if I want to fire him, I can't. Not until I can pay for the cattle. And that may be never."

The man's fingers drummed on the chair arm. "There's a way out," he told her, frowning. "You could resell to me. The contract would be terminated. Then I'd owe him the money and you could let him go."

"Don't tell me, Keith," the girl remarked, "that you'd be interested in buying a herd of condemned cattle?"

Wingate hesitated and seemed uncertain of how to explain.

"I want you to understand me, Jo. When I said those infected steers were a menace to the whole range, I didn't mean the epidemic couldn't be controlled. It can . . . if a man wants to do it. And that's what I'm not sure of . . . that Candler will do his best to stamp it out, to prevent it from reaching other herds. He has you in a position where he can ruin you and get possession of this entire ranch by letting the cattle die and foreclosing for what you owe him. Or he can deliberately throw some of his sick cattle onto my range and infect my herd. That's why we're determined that this thing be brought under control immediately. That's why Sheriff Hale is being harder on you than he would be normally. If any other man were running your iron. . . . But it isn't fair to you, and that's why I don't want to see you suffer this way, needlessly."

He went around the table and, taking her hands, drew her up to him, slim and straight against his own square bulk. "Why do we fight against something we should have done a year ago, Jo?" he said, looking, with a faint smile, into her eyes.

"I . . . I don't understand, Keith." She said that, knowing almost the very words he would use in answering.

"I want you to marry me, Jo." And while her fingers tightened in the rough fabric of his brush coat, he went on: "You've known for years how I felt. And I think . . . maybe I'm being too optimistic . . . that you feel the same way. But somehow we've just let things drift. Everything was so easy for us in K.C. We needed something like this to open our eyes. I want you, Jo! Now! I want you more than life itself!"

"Keith, I don't know. . . ." The girl turned a little and pressed her fingers against her forehead. "It's all confused. It's like looking into a muddy pool and not being able to see the bottom. I don't know what to do."

"That's what Candler has done for you," Wingate said harshly. "What I want to do for you is to clear that pool . . . to show you happiness again. And after things are going smoothly, to take you back home."

Home. . . . Jo felt for a moment the peace, the happiness she had known in Kansas City, a thousand miles from the harsh, clamorous struggle of the American frontier.

She thought of going back, and some of the peace that thought brought her was in her voice as she said: "I do love you, Keith. And we'll be married whenever you say."

Wingate's arms caught her to him. He kissed her, the lamp-light fanning upward upon their faces, pressed close together.

They were standing like that when Sam Candler started up the porch steps. He had turned his pony into the trap, and in his hands was the red tally book. Seeing them, he stopped. He turned after a moment, and stepped quietly into the darkness.

Jo Shelby had long expected a scene with Sam Candler. Because the rest of the crew was at the roundup camp, he ate breakfast in the kitchen, and here Jo came while he was pouring his coffee. She waited until he had finished and sat down. Then she told him bluntly that she was being married, and that he would not be needed on the Lightning after next week.

Sam sipped at the hot coffee. His long face, with its dark tan and its hard shadows, was vacant of emotion. Setting the cup down, he looked evenly at Jo.

He said: "All right. Then Wingate will owe me for the cattle and the contract is broken. That's fine. I'll ride herd on the outfit until you're married. After that, Wingate can do what he likes. I told Dirty Shirt Shelby I'd take care of the place as long as you wanted me to. I can get out with a clear conscience, now."

He got up suddenly, without drinking his coffee, and put on his hat.

Jo said hurriedly: "Wait, Sam. I want to explain something."

"Explain? Who's boss around here . . . me or you?" Candler went out the door, and a few minutes later the sound of his horse's hoofs lifted through the crisp morning air.

As he rode, Candler looked straight ahead, but he was conscious of little that he saw. Jo, married to Wingate. . . . He was both angry and bitterly disappointed. He was ready to admit something to himself that he had evaded a long time. He knew why he hadn't thrown the Lightning over before, why he'd worked as hard to keep the iron together these five years as though it had belonged to him. And why he had almost been hoping beef would take a tumble so that Jo would have to come down here and learn to manage it herself.

He had been hard, because a man had to be hard to survive on this range. But there was that one spot of softness that no man could cut out of himself, and in that spot there was an ache that had been there since the first time he had seen Jo Shelby. It came to him that Jo was doing this to forestall the war she saw coming. If that were so, he supposed it was in part his fault. But it was not his way to be bluffed down by a mangy pack of carrion-hunting lobos. If Jo married Wingate for such a reason as that, she would deserve the misery she found.

Shorty Tylson met him at Piñon Camp, on the bald ridge of a lofty hogback that guarded the Cedar Lodge Springs section, and the undersize, weathered little chunk of cowboy had bad news.

"Five more shorthorns," he said. "Cotton run onto them this morning. He's keepin' them corralled down at the spring till you have a look at them." He left off tinkering with his bridle and looked frowningly at Sam. "Tell you what . . . there's something funny about this epizootic. I never yet saw one that didn't start from some herd passing through. But this 'n' just happened."

"I thought of that, too," Sam Candler said. "That's why I don't aim to quit till the last dog is hung."

They rode down, and Sam looked at the same array of symptoms he had discovered on the other cattle.

He said, at last: "Keep these cows in the corral. I'm going to let the disease run its course and see what happens."

For three days the cattle were kept penned up in the big pole enclosure at the line camp. During this interval a dozen more sick animals were run in by the riders who circled through the timbered cañons and high stony ridges of the section. Candler saw the cows' forelegs swell and blacken, and heard the labored, bubbling breaths they drew with difficulty. On the fourth day two of the beasts died and the rest were mercifully shot.

The count had soared to thirty-two—a total of over $2,000 worth of dead cattle. Candler, although his own interest in the matter was now confined to making Wingate pay for them, dead or alive, felt physically sick when he looked at the lengthening mound under which lay the carcasses. He'd brought these animals through drought and storm, and he'd had faith that they would be the backbone of a new kind of cattle industry. But he was seeing them die off like leppies in a blizzard, and he was helpless to save them.

On the eve of Jo's wedding he saddled his pony.

"Leave three of the boys up here tomorrow to keep an eye on things," he told Shorty, "and the rest of you come down for the wedding. I reckon it'll be around noon. I'll see that the punch is spiked, so at least it'll be worth your ride."

VI

Sam Candler found a lot of strangers about the Lightning headquarters, most of them Mexicans who Wingate had sent over to put the place in trim for the wedding. A dozen dark-skinned women were cleaning and cooking, and the buildings had been given a new coat of whitewash. Candler scarcely recognized the old place. The yard had been spruced up, the heavy mat of oak leaves raked into piles and burned.

Candler awoke depressed the morning of the wedding. A sort of panic grew in his breast, swelling until it suffocated him. *Jo is being married. Jo is being married!* It rang like hammer strokes in his head.

He saw some women about—wives of other ranchers who had come to help the bride with her dress and see that the huge wedding breakfast was properly decked out. But he did not see

Jo. Guests began to arrive, and Candler talked on the porch with the men while the women chattered inside. The cowpunchers rode down from Cedar Lodge Springs, washed up at the stand behind the spring house, and reappeared decked out in clean shirts and polished boots and coats they hadn't worn, some of them, for a year—perhaps longer.

Cotton Riley's face was as red as flame under his blond hair. He sat, smiling stiffly, along the porch rail with the other boys, and Candler asked him: "Shorty coming down?"

"I reckon Shorty slept up at Manzanita Flats last night. Didn't see him after he told us about the clambake. He'll be along."

But the minutes lengthened and the gimlet-eyed little cowpuncher did not appear.

With a high drum roll of hoofs, Keith Wingate appeared with Kenesaw, Sheriff Dunk Hale, and some Antlers cowpunchers. Wingate was at his best in sprucely tailored coat and trousers and fancy-stitched brown boots. His sideburns were trimmed to rapier points. He joined the men on the porch, good-naturedly accepting their banter, but Sam Candler threw his cigarette across the railing and left the group.

Then, suddenly, it was beginning, and everyone was crowding into the spacious parlor. Jo and Keith were standing before Preacher Haskins at the end of the room. Candler could see Jo's face and she looked pale, a little scared. The room fell into silence.

Preacher Haskins opened his book and began to read. " 'Dearly beloved, we are gathered here in the sight of the Lord. . . .' " He looked up, frowning; everyone heard the flutter of hoofs coming into the yard. "Some cuss would have to come in at a time like this," the preacher said, and the men chuckled.

They waited, and in the pause a horse whinnied. The hoofs danced nervously. A swift bolt of apprehension went into Sam

Candler. He looked out the window, and the whole room heard him groan: "My God."

Sam's shoulders pried through the crowd. Reaching the porch, he vaulted the rail and sprinted toward the pony that stood in the middle of the yard, kicking at the thing that hung from one stirrup of the capsized saddle. That thing had once been Shorty Tylson, but what it was now was something much less pleasant and lovable, for most of its head had been left behind on the rocks between here and Cedar Lodge Springs.

They threw the half-crazed horse and cut Shorty's body loose. Sam Candler was among those who lifted him to the bed of a wagon, and thus he was first to discover that a lot of the blood on the body came from a hole in the back of his shirt.

Raising the shirt, Sam found a small, black-edged hole squarely in the center of the cowboy's spine. Sam looked up, not seeing the white, shocked faces about him. All but his own boys and a few Ladron men had gone back to the house.

Sam's voice was husky. "We're going to find out who did it," he said. "And after we do, there's going to be a massacre."

Sheriff Hale came in wheezily: "Now, don't get yourself excited, Sam. There'll be an investigation. Like as not he run into somebody slow-elkin' a beef and they had a shoot-out."

Jo came hurrying from the house with her gown caught up in one hand. Keith was just behind her, remonstrating. Candler stepped forward to stop the girl.

"Go back," he said. "You can't do any good."

"Sam! What happened to him?"

"His horse pitched him and one foot hung up in a stirrup. I reckon he got dragged all the way back from camp."

"Is . . . is that all that happened?"

Candler looked at Wingate with a cold, murderous venom in his eyes. "No. He was shot in the back before he got pitched off."

210

Jo held Wingate's arm, and her eyes were big and dark. "Who would do such a thing?" she asked.

"Shorty had a lot of enemies. Every 'puncher on the ranch has a lot of enemies. I suppose it was one of them."

Wingate said quickly, his syllables short: "Come along, Jo. It's terrible, but we can't do anything for him now. Let's let the preacher finish, and then you can go away from here and forget everything that's happened."

"Let . . . the preacher. . . ." Jo looked at him quickly, with a sort of horror. "After this? Keith, I don't know that I want him to finish. Not until we know what happened to Shorty, anyway. Because I'm sure none of our boys did this."

Sam Candler felt a slow vein of warmth begin to thaw the ice in him. He was looking at Jo's face from the side, and somehow he had never noticed that she had the same aggressive thrust to her chin that old Dirty Shirt Shelby had had.

Wingate's eyes watched her narrowly, his whole manner stiffening. "I don't think I like that, Jo. Obviously Tylson ran into a rustler somewhere and there was gun play." He glanced for one instant at Gil Kenesaw in the crowd, then frowningly back at the girl. "I want you to forget this foolishness. We can't jeopardize our own happiness because of what's happened. Tomorrow is the sheriff's deadline on your cattle. Unless everything goes through as we planned, there's nothing I can do to stop it."

"You mean," Jo said, her lips faintly smiling, "that I can either marry you or fight you."

Wingate frowned, shaking his head. "You're being unreasonable. . . ."

"I think I know what my grandfather would want me to say, Keith. He always made his own terms, and I'll make mine. You can either have me in my own good time, or not at all."

It was Dirty Shirt Shelby's blood boiling up against the blood of Brig Wingate. It was a dangerous mixture that could only brew trouble.

Keith Wingate's jaw hardened. Quietly he said: "Good bye, Jo."

Candler did not see Jo again until all the guests had gone, when the big ranch had settled down to an aching stillness and the cowpunchers were preparing to ride back to camp. Some of the townsmen had taken Shorty off in the wagon, and the bunkhouse was glumly silent except for the sounds of men getting into work clothes.

When Sam was about to go out, he had his brass-mounted Henry in the crook of his elbow and a linen sack full of cartridge boxes in his hand. To the room at large, he remarked: "Better bring all the extra shells you've got. Them cattle may take a lot of killin' when we get around to the job."

Somehow he had expected Jo to spend the rest of the day in her room, weeping. That, he knew, would have been the reaction of the girl who had left Kansas City a few months ago. But the girl who met him at the corral was not the Jo Shelby of K.C. She was in riding skirt and jacket. Her face gave no evidence of weeping. Her eyes were clear, and, if there was distress in them, there was no despair.

Candler reached for a rope from a corral post to catch out her pony.

"I'm making Shorty's apologies for him," he said. "He'd be downright ashamed of breaking up your wedding thataway."

Jo took a deep breath. "If I didn't owe Shorty for anything but that, I'd be forever repaying the debt. He came just in time to show me that I wasn't marrying Keith because I loved him, but because I was afraid."

He had an apology to make in his own behalf, but Jo was going on before he could speak.

"I've been afraid of everything, Sam. Of the country, of the silence, of trouble with the Antlers, even of you."

"Of me?"

"Of you more than anything. Because I knew you represented everything my grandfather stood for. You were a challenge that . . . that frightened me. I was afraid that I wasn't the fighter he'd want me to be, and I didn't want that to be known, even by myself."

Regrets came into Sam Candler, as he thought of the lonely, fearful months Jo must have had, facing alone his scorn and the threats of a dangerous world to whom she was a stranger.

"I've been intolerant, Jo," he said humbly. "I didn't try to understand your side. All I knew was that it meant more than anything, to me, to see the outfit survive."

"And that, now, is all that matters to me," said Jo. "That's why I'm going back up to the camp with you."

"To the camp!" Surprise pounded the exclamation from him. "You're going to stay right here, lady. There's going to be war tomorrow, if Wingate tries to slaughter those beeves. And I'm just as sure he'll try it as I am that he'll have to walk through our lead to do it."

"Would Dirty Shirt Shelby have stayed down here?"

"No, but you ain't. . . ."

"But I'll have to do," said Jo. "Will you get my horse now?"

VII

They reached camp at dark, and Jo had her first taste of camp food—sourdough bread, rank black coffee, and son-of-a-gun stew. The men hunted their blankets early, Candler sending a sentry up to Piñon Camp to watch for a sneak attack during the night.

Breakfast was at dawn. The air was still sharp with frost and a hard white rime lay on the ground. Candler singled out six cowpunchers.

"There's no sense in us waiting for them to start it. You boys start hazing the critters down into Dutchman's Creek and run them out on Manzanita Flats. That will keep them from pot-shooting them from the rims."

He posted others along the low ridges that hemmed in Cedar Lodge Springs. Then he saddled his own horse, hacked off a chunk of sourdough bread, shoved it into his saddlebag, and prepared to ride.

He had not gone far when Jo came following at a lope. Again it was in his mind to send her back, but this time experience dictated silence.

"You're trying to pick up Shorty's trail," she said, aiming an accurate guess. "And I can be more use with you than I can at camp."

Candler said nothing and they rode on.

At Piñon Camp, he found no evidence of the cowboy's having cooked dinner that night. He sought the freshest outtrail, and they followed it, but hoof marks were faint in the sandy, dry earth. Yet it soon became plain that Shorty had been heading toward the outmost bounds of the section in which the cattle were being held.

By a collection of hoof prints beside a scrub oak, Candler knew where Shorty had made his first stop. Locating the semicircular prints of his high heels, he traced a path to a great, sulphide-stained rock that loomed out over the steep slope. Here the cowpuncher must have lain a long time in close scrutiny of the wide cañon yawning below, for the hoof marks gave indication of his pony's having stood for a half hour or more.

"He must have been watching something mighty interesting," Candler told Jo. "Shorty wasn't a man to set still that long."

"I suppose it was just another sick cow," said Jo. "I can see buzzards circling above that bend in the cañon. See, over there!"

"Buzzards?"

Jo pointed. He saw, then, where three of the ominous hunters of carrion swung low above a sweeping turn of the cañon. The timbered cañon side beyond them was gray-green, so that Candler had not seen the buzzards at first glance.

Candler turned back for his horse. "Let's see if he rode on down to that sick cow."

The descent was a matter of forty-five minutes, bringing them at last into the wide bed of the cañon. Where the cañon made a turn, a few rods ahead, the walls of the gorge pressed in, leaving a narrow bosky of sand and rock, with a scattering of oaks and piñon along the creek. They rode slowly along, tracing Shorty's trail in the sand.

Suddenly Jo cried: "Up ahead! It's a dead steer, all right."

Candler sat very straight in the saddle, his eyes seeing more than hers, and he said: "A dead steer and a damn' dead wolf."

She looked sharply at him, then back at the bloated cow shape in the bottom of the dry creek. Candler rode forward, only glancing at the shorthorn steer that had been left three-footed to die miserably against the cutbank. He rode into a copse of black oak, and here Jo joined him beside the sprawled body of big Bart Gillett.

Gillett's beefy body lay on the thick bed of dry leaves behind a thick-boled oak. He lay on his face, a Winchester in his hands. His Stetson lay some distance behind him, and the top of his head had been blasted out by a bullet. Candler looked with a tightening stomach at the corpse, thanking God it was too cold for flies.

Jo turned her head quickly, covering her eyes. Candler was down and slowly circling the body when she found speech.

"Who was it?"

"My old *amigo*, Bart Gillett. He was up here last week to protect his boss' interests. I didn't know how far he was willing to go to protect those interests. It looks like Shorty caught onto it before I did."

That brought Jo's head around. "I don't see what you mean."

"Look here." Candler picked up an object of glass and nickel that lay between the body and the tree. It was a veterinary's hypodermic syringe, a grim-looking affair with a needle half as thick as a lead pencil. Finding it half filled with a murky brown liquor, he let a drop of it fall onto his forefinger, and smelled of it. He rubbed a matchstick in the liquid and watched the white wood turn dark, as if scorched by heat. Candler wiped his finger briskly in the dirt.

"Sulphuric," he said. "Probably Tut Akers's formula. He and Kenesaw have always been thick. I'll trace the syringe down, and, if it's his, we'll give him the same treatment they've been giving these cattle and see whether he doesn't develop blackleg, too."

They walked back to the steer. The tied foreleg was black and swollen, with great festers breaking through the hide, but the free leg was normal. Gingerly Sam pried the animal's jaws apart with a broken oak branch. There was no sign of swelling or redness.

"That's how bad the Wingates have always wanted the Lightning," Candler remarked. "They had this so-called epidemic all worked out before they threw my shorthorns onto your range. After they got the ball rolling, they kept the thing alive by giving the treatment to a few more cows every day and running them up at night to where we couldn't miss them. A sick cow will always head for water, and we found most of them at a spring." He looked up at where Bart Gillett's body was visible in the trees. "I reckon this is as far as Shorty got. He must have spotted Gillett from the rim, and he rode down here to find out what he was doing. Gillett heard him coming and ducked for the trees. When Shorty saw that cow, Gillett knew the jig was up, unless he stopped the cowboy from talking. Like a true Antlers man, he shot him through the back. But Shorty Tylson was a hard son-of-a-gun to kill, and he got off one shot himself. It ain't hard to guess where it went."

Jo bit her lip, the scene made as clear by Candler's words as though they had seen it enacted. Then, in that brief silence, there grew the scuff of iron shoes in the sand. Candler's and Jo's eyes touched for an instant, then the foreman saw three riders come around the near bend of the wash. They were Sheriff Dunk Hale, Gil Kenesaw, and Keith Wingate.

They were close enough so that Wingate's voice was stridently clear. "He couldn't have got much farther. Damn it! You don't suppose they caught him after he killed Tylson?"

"I don't suppose anything," said Kenesaw shortly, "until it happens. But they'd have sprung it on us yesterday if that'd happened."

"Trouble with you cattle fellers," Hale complained, "is that you ain't satisfied until you own every cow in sight. If they find out, you'll be in a nice jackpot."

"We will, eh?" said Kenesaw, his lips slightly emphasizing the *we*. "Who got the syringe for us from Akers, Dunk? You better be damn' sure nobody gets in any jackpot, or you'll be threshing around in it, too."

They were still 200 feet off, and Candler whispered to Jo: "Run for it! I'll hold their fire till you find your horse and head out. Bring the boys back, if you can. But get out!"

It was in the wideness of Jo's eyes and the pallor of her face that showed she was frightened. But she stood resolutely at his side and whispered: "I'll stay with you, Sam. Maybe you can bluff them down."

"These lads won't bluff," Candler jerked out, and he gave her an urgent shove toward the trees. "They'll see us in another fifteen seconds. On your way."

"I've done nothing but run since I got here, and it's got me nowhere. My place is right here with you, and this time I'm not going to run."

Candler looked at her and knew she meant it. He drew her with him to a boulder half eaten from the bank by roiling spring floods, and here they knelt, with Candler laying his Colt on the sand and raising his rifle to his shoulder, the girl taking up a handful of the shells he dug from his chaps pockets.

The riders came around the bend into the middle of the arroyo.

Candler's voice, rising suddenly, put each man back against the cantle.

"This is as far as Gillett got, boys . . . and it's as far as you get! Drag 'em or reach!"

Strangely it was Hale whose .45 flashed in the cold sunlight, Hale whose horse reared as the Colt blasted twice, the booming echoes mixing grotesquely with the *whine* of lead spinning off the rock that shielded Sam Candler and Jo. Then the fat lawman piled out of the saddle and ducked for the protective cutbank that thrust itself between them. Candler let him almost reach the shoulder before he gently squeezed the trigger. The impact of the heavy slug knocked Hale down, and there he lay in the sand with his neck broken, stirring for a while, and then relaxing.

Kenesaw, quitting the saddle to seek the same shelter, fired once on the run, but his bullet was wild and the one Sam Candler threw after him likewise missed its target. Suddenly, then, the arroyo was quiet; only the whispering of the wind in the trees, the sound of horses running down the wash, came between hunted and hunters. Presently Wingate's voice came, stiffly.

"We mean to get him, Jo. You'll only be jeopardizing your own life to stay with him."

Jo did not answer.

Gathering confidence, Wingate argued: "Nothing has changed between you and me. We can still leave all this behind. But not if you're determined to pick the losing side!"

With Candler's revolver, Jo made her answer. The crashing echoes of the shot poured down the barranca and a puff of dust exploded from the bank.

"As my grandfather would say," Jo called through the echoes, "I always pick the winner!"

There was silence again. But, through it, Sam detected the sounds of a man moving across the sand. He had his eye riveted to the shoulder that hid them, and the warm stock of the gun was against his cheek. Nothing happened, and at length he discovered what must be going on.

"Kenesaw's going back down the wash," he grunted. "He'll come out in the trees and coyote back to Gillett's body. They'll have us between them, then."

He heard those small crawling sounds die, and the urgency of the moment pressed hard upon him. If Kenesaw reached his objective, they were trapped. He knew, despite Wingate's proposition, that only Jo's death, too, would give Wingate the protection he must have.

He asked Jo after a moment: "Can you shoot a rifle?"

"I can shoot it. But I don't know whether I could hit a barn."

Candler traded guns with her. "When you see Kenesaw, start pouring lead at him. He'll take cover, and that may give us the time we need."

Fifteen agonizingly slow minutes crept by. Candler's nerves were like hot wires. They contracted suddenly as he saw a man's Stetson move behind a screen of gray buckthorn. He pointed it out to the girl. "He'll break past that brush in a minute and hunt a tree. Snap one at him when he does. Keep on firing so that he can't risk a shot at us."

Candler fixed his own gaze on the cutbank that hid Keith Wingate. The roar of Jo's rifle came so startlingly that he leaped from cover like a scared rabbit. He saw the Antlers ramrod fling himself on the ground. In the next moment Candler was on his way.

Wingate was being careful. He had not showed himself, and Sam Candler prayed that he would continue to play his cards cautiously. Candler jumped Hale's body and kept running. He was almost to the bend when Keith Wingate rose from his ambush. His rifle was directed toward Jo, and in the split second it took him to swing the weapon Sam Candler fired. Struck high in the shoulder, Wingate staggered back, coming up against the bank. His face was tallow-colored, and there was that small, neat hole punched in the tan fabric of his coat. Again he put the Winchester to his shoulder, and once more Sam fired.

With Wingate down, Candler swung back to find Gil Kenesaw. His glance, flashing among the trees, was arrested by the huddled shape lying precisely where the ramrod had fallen at Jo's first shot. But there was caution in his advance from the arroyo to where Kenesaw lay.

It was caution wasted. Kenesaw had a hole in the side of his head and another in his shoulder.

Jo was sitting in the sand at the base of the boulder. Around her, the sand was littered with empty cartridges. The rifle lay across her lap, but her hands had fallen from it in a surge of relief after Candler had straightened from Kenesaw's body.

"Did you say you couldn't hit a barn?" Sam asked her.

"Did I . . . hit him?"

Candler helped her up. "He was dead when he landed."

Jo looked strangely at the rifle. "I haven't shot one in years. I had the feeling that I was only sitting there, and someone else was doing the shooting. Someone who had fired a gun so many times it was as natural as breathing."

"That," said Candler soberly, "was Dirty Shirt. I've always believed he was still wandering around these hills, as cantankerous and as dangerous to meddle with as ever. Sort of protecting his interests until a Shelby showed up."

"Then he can go back to his rest," Jo said. "Because this Shelby has come to stay."

Candler brought the horses. As he helped her into the saddle, he lingered a moment, looking up at her and still holding her hand. "I wonder if it would matter to him if the Shelby changed her name, as long as she married somebody he'd sort of picked out himself?"

And all Jo said was: "He's always had his way so far, hasn't he?"

ABOUT THE AUTHOR

Frank Bonham, in a career that spanned five decades, achieved excellence as a noted author of young adult fiction and detective and mystery fiction, as well as making significant contributions to Western fiction. By 1941 his fiction was already headlining Street and Smith's *Western Story* and by the end of the decade his Western novels were being serialized in *The Saturday Evening Post.* His first Western, *Lost Stage Valley* (1948), was purchased as the basis for the motion picture, *Stage to Tucson* (Columbia, 1951) with Rod Cameron as Grif Holbrook and Sally Eilers as Annie Benson. "I have tried to avoid," Bonham once confessed, "the conventional cowboy story, but I think it was probably a mistake. That is like trying to avoid crime in writing a mystery book. I just happened to be more interested in stagecoaching, mining, railroading. . . ." Yet, notwithstanding, it is precisely the interesting—and by comparison with the majority of Western novels—exotic backgrounds of Bonham's novels that give them an added dimension. He was highly knowledgeable in the technical aspects of transportation and communication in the 19th-Century American West. In introducing these backgrounds into his narratives, especially when combined with his firm grasp of idiomatic Spanish spoken by many of his Mexican characters, his stories and novels are elevated to a higher plane in which the historical sense of the period is always very much in the forefront. This historical aspect of his Western fiction early drew accolades from reviewers so that on one occasion the *Long Beach Press Telegram* predicted that "when the time comes to find an author who can best fill the gap in Western fiction left by Ernest Haycox, it may be that Frank Bonham will serve well." Among his best Western novels are *Snaketrack* (1952), *Night Raid* (1954), *The Feud at Spanish Ford* (1954), and *Last Stage West* (1959). *The Dark Border* will be his next Five Star Western.

ABOUT THE EDITOR

Bill Pronzini was born in Petaluma, California. His earliest Western fiction was published under his own name and a variety of pseudonyms in Zane Grey Western Magazine. Among his most notable Western novels are *The Last Days of Horse-Shy Halloran* (1987) and *Firewind* (1989). He is also the editor of numerous Western story collections, including *Under the Burning Sun: Western Stories* (Five Star Westerns, 1997) by H.A. DeRosso, *Renegade River: Western Stories* (Five Star Westerns, 1998) by Giff Cheshire, and *Tracks in the Sand* by H.A. DeRosso (Five Star Westerns, 2001). His own Western story collection, *All the Long Years* (Five Star Westerns, 2001), was followed by *Burgade's Crossing* (Five Star Westerns, 2003), *Quincannon's Game* (Five Star Westerns, 2005), and *Coyote and Quarter-Moon* (Five Star Westerns, 2006). His latest Five Star Western is *Crucifixion River* with Marcia Muller.